"What did you say?"

"I said I've joined the Tennessee militia. We're in the middle of a war, and General Jackson says it's our duty to help keep this country safe. He has so many great ideas. If all of the members of Congress would listen to him, I have no doubt the British would already have been routed."

Rebekah's dreams crashed around her as the meaning of his words sank in. Asher had not come to ask for her hand in marriage. He had come to tell her good-bye. She shook her head in denial, backing away from him. "You're. . .going away? How could you do this to me—to us?"

DIANE ASHLEY, a "town girl" born and raised in Mississippi, has worked more than twenty years for the House of Representatives. She rediscovered a thirst for writing, was led to a class taught by Aaron McCarver, and became a founding member of the Bards of Faith. Visit her at www.bardsoffaith.homestead.com

AARON McCARVER is a transplanted Mississippian who was raised in the mountains near Dunlap, Tennessee. He loves his jobs of teaching at two Christian colleges and editing for Barbour Publishing. A member of ACFW, he is coauthor with Gilbert Morris of the bestselling series, The Spirit of Appalachia.

Don't miss out on any of our super romances. Write to us at the following address for information on our newest releases and club information.

Heartsong Presents Readers' Service
PO Box 721
Uhrichsville, OH 44683

Or visit www.heartsongpresents.com

Under the Tulip Poplar

Diane Ashley and Aaron McCarver

Heartsong Presents

From Aaron:
To Gilbert Morris, a true legend: None of the wonderful opportunities that have come to me in the Christian publishing industry would have happened without your special help and guidance. Thank you for all you have done for me, for your special friendship...and for finally redeeming the name "Aaron." With special love to Johnnie and Lynn, too.

From Diane:

To Vicki Tyner Joyce and Mitchell Harry Tyner: No one could have better siblings. Together we have faced many challenges, and I deeply appreciate the times you were there for me to lean on. Daddy was right, you know—blood really is thicker than water

In loving memory:
Weldon Harry Tyner, Jr.—September 12, 1933–September 26, 1995
Dorothy Gene McKinley Tyner—April 16, 1934–April 30, 1997

A note from the Authors:
We love to hear from our readers! You may correspond with us by writing:

Diane Ashley and Aaron McCarver
Author Relations
PO Box 721
Uhrichsville, OH 44683

ISBN 978-1-60260-519-0

UNDER THE TULIP POPLAR

Copyright © 2009 by Diane Ashley and Aaron McCarver. All rights reserved. Except for use in any review, the reproduction or utilization of this work in whole or in part in any form by any electronic, mechanical, or other means, now known or hereafter invented, is forbidden without the permission of Heartsong Presents, an imprint of Barbour Publishing, Inc., PO Box 721, Uhrichsville, Ohio 44683.

All scripture quotations are taken from the King James Version of the Bible.

All of the characters and events in this book are fictitious. Any resemblance to actual persons, living or dead, or to actual events is purely coincidental.

Our mission is to publish and distribute inspirational products offering exceptional value and biblical encouragement to the masses.

PRINTED IN THE U.S.A.

prologue

Taylor farm outside Nashville, Tennessee,
Mid-September 1813

"Rebekah, send Eleanor out to gather the eggs this morning. I need you to help your pa with the corn. He got behind when he went to that rally last week."

Rebekah Taylor watched as her ma plucked little Donny out of his crib and cradled him in her arms. She could understand her ma's happy expression. Donny was an adorable bundle. They all spent time cooing over him to get him to show his tiny dimples.

Like her, he took his coloring from their pa—light blond hair and eyes as brown as a hickory nut. Eleanor looked more like Ma with her curly brown hair and hazel eyes. Rebekah often wished she had inherited a few curls of her own, but her hair only curled if they applied a hot iron to it, and then only for a few hours before stubbornly straightening out again.

"Hurry up now. The weather is getting cooler, and we don't need to risk losing our crop to an early freeze." Martha Taylor smiled as Donny gurgled, one tiny hand swinging through the air as if he were waving good-bye.

"Yes, ma'am." Rebekah tried to keep the disappointment out of her voice. If she was out in the field with her pa, she might miss seeing Asher if he came for a visit. And she had the feeling he was planning to stop by. The weather was gorgeous, and besides, it had been nearly a week since his last visit. She didn't know how much longer she could keep their news secret.

Not that her parents didn't suspect the truth. She and

Asher had been sitting together in church for almost a year now. Everyone knew that the two of them had been keeping company since last spring when he came back from the College of William and Mary in Virginia. But how was he supposed to see her if she couldn't even stay home and wait for him? She would have asked the question out loud except for the distracted look on her ma's face. Pastor's words from last Sunday rang in her ears: *"Every Christian has the duty of putting the needs of others first."* Pastor taught that was the way to make certain all needs were met according to God's plan.

Rebekah placed the egg basket into the waiting hands of her six-year-old sister. Eleanor's eyes sparkled, and she grinned widely, showing the gap between her front teeth. She was nearly dancing with the excitement of her new responsibility. The basket dangled from one hand, and she held her skirt up with the other as she fairly skipped out of the cabin.

Rebekah sighed and carefully removed the apron she'd donned that morning in an attempt to look more dignified in case of a caller. It would never survive a day of field work. She folded it and placed it in the chest at the end of her cot. Another sigh. How could she manage to be where Asher could find her and still do as her parents wished?

Slow footsteps took her to the door. Rebekah sighed once more.

"Whatever is the matter with you? You sound like one of those fancy Scottish musicians. Remember? What did they call those big instruments?"

Rebekah thought back to the magical night. Her whole family had spent a long weekend in Nashville while her pa bartered with the local merchants. How excited she had been when her pa had allowed Asher's parents to pay for all of them to attend a special concert. She remembered the way Asher's azure eyes looked in the dark theater and the feel of his strong arm under her hand as he helped her to her seat. A blush suffused her cheeks. "I. . .they were bagpipes."

"That's right." Her ma turned to look at Rebekah. "And why are you blushing? Could it be thoughts of a certain young man. . . ?"

Rebekah ducked her head and reached for the door. She was outside and halfway across the yard before her ma could finish the gentle teasing. It was so good to be alive on a beautiful day like today, even if she might have to miss seeing Asher. Maybe he would come looking for her. She halted for a moment as another thought struck her—maybe that was the real reason Ma had sent her out to work in the fields with Pa. Maybe it would be better if Asher had to come looking for her.

❧

Asher Landon, Esq., encouraged his horse along the rutted track toward the Taylor homestead. The long, fifteen-mile trip from Nashville had seemed easier today because he was anxious to share his news with Rebekah. She would be so excited. At least he hoped so.

After the rally in Nashville last week, he and his pa had debated Andrew Jackson's plan day and night. The general was very convincing. And he had a lot of experience, even if President Madison did not want to give the man a chance.

It was a shame how those pompous windbags back East tried to control things they didn't understand. Like how they'd sent General Jackson to defend New Orleans last year, then changed their minds when he got to Natchez and told him to disband the militia. But the general had showed them. He'd refused to abandon his men so far from home. He'd brought them all back, even giving up his own horses so that the wounded and sick would have easier transportation. No wonder they called him Old Hickory. That march had shown everyone how tough General Jackson was.

How Asher wished he could have been part of that campaign. But he'd been off at college. Now he was a man. He was ready and eager to do his duty for his country.

General Jackson had spoken long and hard about that very thing last week. Asher agreed with everything the man said. If they did not all stand against the English and their Indian allies, they would end up losing their hard-won independence. He was not about to stand around and let his home and family be threatened. Especially after the horrific massacre down at Fort Mims. Those Creek Indians needed to be trounced, and General Jackson was the man to do the job.

Asher pressed his knees together, urging his horse to hurry a bit as he spotted Rebekah's cabin. From amble to canter to gallop, he hurried to reach the cabin and the girl he hoped would one day become his wife.

When he reached the yard, he dismounted and looped the reins around a sapling. Always aware of his appearance, Asher took a moment to dust off his trousers and straighten his jacket. He glanced longingly toward the stream that gurgled between leafy poplars to one side of the cabin. Maybe he could coax Rebekah into dipping him a cool drink. It would give him an excuse to get closer to her. The very thought made his heart speed up a bit. He couldn't remember a time when he had not loved Rebekah Taylor and planned to make her his wife. But sometimes, personal desires needed to be set aside for greater ideals. There would be time for them to marry and start a family as soon as he got back.

❧

"Good afternoon, Mr. Taylor, Miss Rebekah."

Asher's familiar voice brought a gasp to Rebekah's throat. She straightened and tugged her bonnet back onto her head, tucking strands of hair under it with an impatient hand. She should never have let it slip and hang down her back. No matter that the late-morning sun had made her face as hot as a bed of coals. Now she would probably have a dozen new freckles she would have to bleach with lemon juice. She wanted to cry in exasperation. Why did she have to look so. . . so frowsy?

Asher dismounted, looking every inch the dapper young businessman. Just seeing his straight shoulders and easy smile made her heart beat faster. She never grew tired of looking at him. He was the one who held her heart and occupied most of her thoughts.

Growing up near him, she had admired Asher's honesty and integrity as well as his innate kindness. She had turned to him with every problem, and he'd always managed to find a solution. Her heart had broken when his parents insisted on sending him away to college. But now he was back, and they could begin their life together.

As he strode across the rows toward Rebekah and her pa, her gaze drank in his snowy white neckcloth and stylish blue coat. These days, Asher always looked like a fashion plate—as if he were ready to attend a society picnic or a tea party. The color of his coat was reflected in his eyes—eyes that sometimes reminded her of a cloudless summer sky, and at others of a picture of the Atlantic Ocean she had seen hanging in Aunt Dolly's parlor in Nashville.

Her pa's dry voice caught Rebekah's attention. "I wonder what a young man might be doing this far from Nashville on a fine autumn day." His right eyebrow rose up as he glanced from Asher to Rebekah.

Asher cleared his throat and thrust out a hand. "My pa sends his greetings, sir. We missed seeing you at the rally last week." As the two men shook hands, Asher looked over Pa's shoulder, and his smile widened ever so slightly.

Rebekah could not keep from returning his smile. Suddenly, it did not matter as much that she was hot and tired from working beside her pa all morning. It only mattered that Asher had come. And he was smiling. The world seemed to fade away.

As if from a distance, she heard her pa's voice and recognized the gentle humor in his tone. "I believe I'll go back to the house and see if your ma still has one of those biscuits left over from breakfast."

"Do you want me to come with you, Pa?" Rebekah held her breath, hoping he would turn down her offer.

"Seems to me that you need to finish that row, Rebekah. Perhaps Asher could help you gather the rest of the corn."

"It would be my honor, sir."

"I'll not be very far away. So be certain to mind your manners, you two." Her pa hummed a lilting melody as he turned to leave.

Asher reached for the half-empty basket at the end of the row. "Thank you, sir. We'll only be a few moments."

Rebekah could feel the color rising in her cheeks. Why did Pa have to be so old-fashioned? He knew Asher was a gentleman and could be trusted to treat her with respect. Blindly, she grabbed the nearest stalk and stripped an ear of corn from it.

Silence filled the air between her and Asher for several minutes as they worked side by side. Then it happened. They both reached for the same stalk. Their hands brushed against each other. Rebekah caught her breath, and then when she tried to draw her hand away, Asher wrapped his fingers around hers. Her heart stuttered to a halt and seemed to lose its rhythm. Her breathing grew ragged, and she had a difficult time concentrating.

"We have to talk, Rebekah. There's something I have to tell you."

This was it! She was about to hear the words she'd been dreaming of for weeks. What would she say? Should she pull her hand away? Or leave it in his? But the feel of their hands tenderly clasped together felt so right. There had been very little private time between them. Only whispered compliments and tender glances. But she had known for several weeks that Asher wanted to ask her to marry him.

She wondered if he had talked to her pa yet. That might explain why Pa had been willing to leave them alone for a few minutes. Had Pa given his permission? But when could Asher have spoken to him? She would have known if he'd come to their home.

Rebekah tugged the hand he had captured, disappointed when he allowed her to pull it away without resistance. His eyes narrowed, and he turned his head up. She noticed his square chin and the way his Adam's apple bobbed up and down in the folds of his neckcloth before she allowed her own gaze to sweep the midday sky.

The sun had bleached most of the color away, leaving the sky pale. A flock of geese winged a southerly path across the sky as she waited for Asher to continue. Should she say something? Had he changed his mind? Should she have let him keep holding her hand? Had he lost his courage?

Asher ran a finger around the collar of his shirt and looked at her once again. "It's quite hot for September."

"Yes, I suppose so." Rebekah turned back to the corn, somewhat surprised to realize they had completed the row. It was time to go back to the cabin. "How are your parents doing?"

"They're fine, thank you. They send their compliments and told me to ask you to consider visiting again in the near future."

Rebekah held her breath. If his parents were sending messages like that, they must have given their blessing. "I will see. I'm not sure when Ma and Pa will return to Nashville. But please tell your family I miss them and would love to visit."

"Yes, well. . ." His voice drifted off, and he looked over her shoulder. "Let's go sit under our tree."

Her heart turned over. How she loved Asher. He was such a romantic. "Their tree" was the tall, shady tulip poplar that towered over one end of the field. They had often played there as young children.

As they walked toward the broad-leafed tree that's leaves had just started to turn yellow-gold around the edges, Asher continued their conversation. "Did I tell you that Pa has talked with General Jackson about his idea for a new kind of banking system?"

Rebekah twisted a hand in the skirt of her dress. What did she care about banking?

But Asher apparently did not recognize her frustration. He continued talking about his pa's plans and the economic challenges faced by the nation as it struggled to define itself apart from the English Crown.

Rebekah nodded as her mind wandered to the familiar visions that occupied most of her waking hours. She could see Asher entering the front door of their comfortable home and giving her a quick hug before being swamped with loving hugs and kisses from their children. She would stand back and smile, waiting until their eyes met and his hand reached for hers. They would walk together to a dining table filled with fresh vegetables, meat, and a heady assortment of fruits. After dinner, she would darn clothes by the fireplace while he spoke of his challenging job. They would gather the children together, and Asher would read to them from God's Holy Word. Then they would all pray for God's blessings and thank Him for leading them safely through another day. . . .

". . .has such a vision for our country. And I think it's time for me to fight for our freedom. Don't you agree?"

Rebekah drew her mind away from her daydreams. "What did you say?"

"I said I've joined the Tennessee militia. We're in the middle of a war, and General Jackson says it's our duty to help keep this country safe. He has so many great ideas. If all of the members of Congress would listen to him, I have no doubt the British would already have been routed."

Rebekah's dreams crashed around her as the meaning of his words sank in. Asher had not come to ask for her hand in marriage. He had come to tell her good-bye. She shook her head in denial, backing away from him. "You're. . .going away? How could you do this to me—to us?"

Asher's eyes darkened. "I know you don't mean what you're saying, Rebekah. My pa fought for our freedom, the same as yours. You and I both know I owe a duty as an American citizen to heed the call to arms. Our very lifestyles are at risk. Everything that you and I have was wrested from English tyranny only a few decades ago. If we ignore the needs of our nation, how can our country survive?"

Tears flooded her eyes. It was fine to talk about patriotism and sacrifice until it became personal. What Asher was talking about was not just some fine ideal to be discussed and argued by the menfolk. This was *her* love, *her* life, *her* future. And it was being destroyed before it could even begin. In an instant everything had changed. All of her dreams and hopes lay shattered. Rebekah balled her fists and pressed them against her eyelids. She would not cry.

She felt his hands on her shoulders, and she lost the precarious control over her emotions. Hot tears pushed their way past her knuckles. On some level, she knew his arms had wrapped around her. Asher was rocking her like a baby and whispering words of comfort and endearment into her ear. But mere words could neither fill the emptiness nor calm the fear that had settled in her heart.

one

March 1814

Rebekah waved to Eleanor and Ma as Pa clucked his tongue and Old Bess ambled forward. The wagon jerked, marking the beginning of her exciting adventure. So why did she feel like crying along with her little sister, whose face was hidden in Ma's skirts? For a minute, Rebekah wanted to tell Pa to stop. No matter that Aunt Dolly was sick and needed help. She could not go through with leaving. She stretched a hand out toward his arm. But then, looking up at the taut expression on his face, she let the hand fall back to her lap.

She twisted in her seat as the wagon turned a curve on the track. "I'll be back before you know it." She forced the words past the large lump that had wedged itself in her throat.

"Are you all right, Becka?" Pa's brown gaze, so wise and gentle, made her want to weep even more. He looked sad, infected with the same sorrow that had flooded every member of the family.

"Yes, sir."

"Your ma and I discussed this at great length over the past week. We're going to miss you dreadfully, but your aunt Dolly needs our help. Since your uncle George passed away, she has no family but us. She's been quite sick for a month, and now, one of her maids quit to move to Knoxville with her husband." He shook his head. "My sister does not trust that anyone else is capable of hiring competent help, so she has asked if we would allow you to come stay with her for a while."

Rebekah nodded. Her whole life had turned upside down

14

since last fall. First, Asher had not asked her to marry him. Then he'd left. He was gone—still fighting the Indians, or the British, or whoever it was they thought they had to defeat. She prayed for him every day.

Before the beginning of the new year, there had been little news, only the report from Mr. Partain, who owned the farm over the rise, that there had been a large group of volunteers. Nearly twice as many as expected. But not to worry; they had sufficient provisions to last for a considerable length of time. When they learned of the need to send more supplies, she and Ma had contributed baskets of cornmeal and flour, as well as jars of honey and canned tomatoes.

She sure wished she could tell Andrew Jackson a thing or two. He was the reason everyone had gotten so riled up. She had seen the famous general once while they were in Nashville, but her parents had not sought out his acquaintance. He was a good-looking man, tall and proud, even if he was old. Probably as old as her pa. But no matter his age, the man undoubtedly had a silver tongue. One rousing speech from him, and Asher had decided to answer the call to arms instead of wrapping his arms around her.

A sigh filled her chest, and Rebekah let it escape quietly. No need to upset Pa. She already knew he didn't really want her to leave to stay with Aunt Dolly. Last week, she had heard her parents arguing late into the night. But Aunt Dolly was sick, and Ma could not go tend to her. Eleanor was too young and Pa had to work the land, so Rebekah was the logical choice. Ma had explained the situation to her two days ago during breakfast.

At first, Rebekah had been excited. Staying in Nashville would be a dream come true. All of the shops, the people, the excitement of being in the midst of things. She would know all the news well ahead of her parents. Everyone in Nashville heard about current events from the traffic along the river.

Unlike at home, where news came weeks late, if at all, the newspaper would likely be delivered to Aunt Dolly's home the day it was printed.

What would life be like at Aunt Dolly's? She remembered visiting her aunt last year and being awed by the luxurious furnishings and modern conveniences that her ma's sister enjoyed. She even had running water in the house—a long-handled pump that could make water gush out faster than a river during the spring melt.

No more buckets to be filled at the creek. Rebekah flexed her hand. Even with a cloth wrapped around the handle, a heavy bucket could raise blisters when it had to be carried into the cabin several times a day. That was a chore she would not miss.

She would miss other things, however. She would miss sleeping next to Eleanor and teasing her younger sister. She would miss playing with the baby and practicing her reading and writing with Pa's guidance. She would even miss sewing and cooking and making jams and jellies with Ma.

But how silly she was being. Aunt Dolly most likely sewed. She might even have some new patterns Rebekah could use to embroider a pair of pillowcases for Ma and Pa. If she could barter something for material, she could also make a pinafore for her little sister and stitch Eleanor's initials on it. What a grand scene it would be when her family arrived to fetch her. Aunt Dolly would be recovered from her illness and doting on her. Everyone would be very impressed with her skills, and Aunt Dolly would be reluctant to let her return home.

The front wheel of the wagon hit a rut, forcing Rebekah to abandon her daydreams and grasp the edge of her seat.

"I want you to mind your manners while you are staying with your aunt Dolly. I do not want to hear reports of your acting like anything but the most gently bred young lady in Nashville. Always get one of the servants to accompany you when you leave the house, no matter how close your destination. There are dangers around every corner when you're staying in a bustling city like Nashville. You cannot imagine the types of characters who would love to prey on an innocent country girl."

"Of course, Pa. I'll be very careful." Rebekah couldn't keep the note of surprise from her voice. She'd seen no evidence of troublemakers when they'd traveled to Nashville last year.

Looping the reins over his left hand, her pa reached his right hand under her chin and raised her face toward his. "I know you mean that. But you're very young and innocent, my dear. I don't know if we did you a service to keep you so insulated from the dangers of city living."

Rebekah put her hand over his larger one and squeezed it. "You and Ma have done an excellent job of raising me. You've taught me to rely on God and His instructions in the Bible. I won't let you down."

"You could never let me or your ma down, honey. We love you and only want the best for you. Your ma thinks this visit may be an excellent opportunity for you, as well as a boon for her sister. Aunt Dolly has apparently decided it is time for you to think of marriage and raising a family of your own."

Rebekah blushed at his words and looked away at the rolling hills, dotted here and there with the remnants of last week's dusting of snow. "I'm nearly seventeen years old. Wasn't that how old Ma was when she married you?"

Pa nodded and returned his attention to the road ahead of them. "But I didn't realize then quite how young she was. I guess you'll always be my baby."

"You don't have anything to worry about. You know I'm waiting for Asher Landon to return from fighting. I'm not likely to have my head turned by anyone in Nashville. Besides, I'll be spending all my time nursing Aunt Dolly back to health. If she gets better soon, I might even be traveling back home within a month. And if I'm not, maybe you can bring everyone for a visit."

"We will see. . . ." His voice faded away as they topped a hill.

The sun's weak winter rays made it hard for her to make out the gray shape some distance ahead of them. "What's that?"

"I don't know." Her pa reached under the seat for his musket and swung it across his knees.

Rebekah could feel her heart racing as their wagon slowly gained on the dark shadow. When it was a couple of hundred yards away, she giggled her relief. "It's only an empty cart."

"Yes, but where is its driver? The horses? Why is it sitting out here unattended?" Pa slowed their wagon to a crawl. "I want you to get in the back. Get under the blanket, and don't come out unless I tell you to."

"But, Pa—"

"Don't argue with me." His curt tone got her attention.

Without further protest, Rebekah gathered her skirts and climbed over the seat. She shifted her baggage and the crates of corn around until she had made an opening she could squeeze into.

"Are you hidden?"

"Yes, sir." Rebekah pulled a horse blanket up and over her. It was warm and stuffy under the woolen material. She fought the urge to sneeze and strained her ears to hear over the creaking of the wagon wheels. After a few moments, she heard the unmistakable thunder of several horses racing toward them. Why didn't Pa speed up? If *she* were driving, Old Bess would be halfway to Nashville by now.

The hoofbeats drew closer until Rebekah was sure the riders would run right over Pa. Then the sound changed to stomping paws and whinnies. The wagon came to a complete stop and shifted slightly, indicating her pa had stood up to face the horsemen. She heard his calm voice question the riders about their intentions. The answer was a series of staccato syllables. Indians!

Her scalp tingled with remembered stories of Indian braves and their trophies. She could not make out exactly what was said because the flaps of her bonnet had been mashed against her ears by the blanket that covered her. Rebekah wished she had the courage to pull the bonnet off or even stand up and face the Indians. But she dared not move an inch.

After what sounded like a heated exchange, the Indians rode away. Her pa clucked to the horse, and they ambled down the road.

"Stay where you are. I don't want them to know you're here." His voice was gruff with repressed fear. She recognized the tone from past incidents. Out on the untamed frontier, danger lurked at every bend of the road.

Rebekah gritted her teeth and remained hidden for what seemed an eternity. The road grew rougher, causing the wagon to lurch uncontrollably and throw her against the rough edges of the wooden baskets at her back. By the time this was over, she would be a mass of bruises and splinters. Finally, Pa brought the wagon to a halt. She felt the blanket being pulled away.

"Are you all right?"

"What happened? What was that all about?"

Pa's face was creased with worry. "A group of Cherokee braves claimed the travelers who drove that cart were ambushed and left for dead by a band of Creek Indians."

Rebekah could feel the blood draining from her face. Since the massacre at Fort Sims near Mobile, there had been more and more stories of Indian attacks on innocent farmers and traders, although the area around Nashville had remained relatively peaceful. Rebekah prayed that was not changing. Some of the Indian tribes had joined forces with the English and, some said, the Spanish. All three groups seemed determined to crush the expansion of the United States.

Rebekah knew God was in control, but sometimes she thought how wonderful it would be if He would just step in with a few miracles and stop all the terrible killing. With a shake of her head, she looked around, only now realizing that she did not recognize their surroundings. "Where are we?"

"The Cherokee warned me to get off the road and make haste to Nashville. You'll have to get back up here and look out for trouble."

Taking a deep breath for courage, Rebekah gathered her skirts and clambered back onto the seat. "It's a good thing you taught me how to use your musket."

❧

Asher was on guard duty again. He marched wearily forward, turned, retraced his steps, and then turned back once more. Evening was beginning to darken the landscape. Another day in the unforgiving wilderness. At least it was no longer as bitterly cold as it had been. After the desertion of so many of the troops in January, it seemed that Jackson's command was doomed to failure. But the warmer weather had brought provisions, new soldiers, and defeat of the enemy.

After the resounding victory over the Creek Indians at Horseshoe Bend, the talk was that the Indians no longer had the weapons, support, or manpower to mount an attack against innocent settlers. They had been decimated. Remembering the carnage that followed the battle still tended to make him feel ill. Six months of fierce battles and forced marches without sufficient rations had hardened him so much that few things had the power to make him queasy anymore. But the savagery that had been visited upon the Indians had been beyond vicious—as brutal as the attack on Fort Mims that had precipitated this campaign. It proved to Asher that any man, white or Indian, could be overcome by bloodlust. He was thankful that his faith in God had helped him resist the temptation to take revenge on the hapless survivors.

"Do you see that man?" The quiet voice of a nearby soldier distracted him from his somber thoughts.

Asher looked at the soldier before turning his attention in the direction indicated. Two soldiers were escorting an Indian across the center of the camp. "Who is he?"

"Someone said he's Chief Red Eagle come to surrender to General Jackson."

Asher looked curiously at the tall, fair-skinned man being led toward General Jackson's tent. He wore his hair long in the style of an Indian and was bare from the waist up, but somehow, he didn't fit with Asher's idea of an Indian chief. "He's the one who led the massacre at Fort Mims? Except for his dress, he doesn't even look like an Indian, much less a chieftain."

"They say he's only half Indian." The soldier spat at the ground next to Asher's boot, obviously to show his disgust and contempt for the chief. "His pa was a Scots trader."

The Indian walked ahead of his horse, on which a deer had been strapped. For some reason, he stopped and looked toward them, his piercing gaze seeming to see right through Asher. With a gasp of dismay, the gossiping soldier slipped off into the gathering gloom.

His gaze caught by the stranger, Asher refused to look away. He would not be cowed by an Indian, no matter what title he might hold.

Another soldier confronted Red Eagle, and after a brief altercation, the two entered General Jackson's tent.

Asher sighed and once again began his slow walk back and forth across the camp. Sixty-four paces to the tall oak. Turn. Sixty-four paces to the edge of the pine forest. Turn.

A tiny sliver of moon appeared on the eastern horizon, and Asher's stomach rumbled. Given the amount of noise it was making, he probably wouldn't hear an Indian attack until an arrow pierced his chest. He should have brought a biscuit to assuage his hunger. A bead of sweat trickled down his back. Turn.

"You're being summoned to the general's tent." The voice of his captain interrupted the monotony of Asher's measured paces. "I've brought Johnson to relieve you."

Asher didn't know whether to be excited or worried. Why would General Jackson want to see him? He didn't even know the general knew his name. Had he done something wrong? He tried to be so careful to meet and even exceed every order he was given. He'd volunteered to remain with the troops even when his tour of duty had officially ended in January. Many had chosen to return home, and Asher had wanted to see his family—and Rebekah—again, but he was here to serve a purpose for God and his country. He would not leave his duty incomplete, even for the chance to be reunited with his love.

His mind went back over the events of the day. He'd risen from his pallet at first light, made up his bedroll, and dug out the battered coffeepot that his pa had sent with him last October when this campaign began. He'd been lucky enough to trap a rabbit yesterday and had traded part of the fresh meat for a double handful of chicory-laced coffee grounds. The coffee he'd made this morning was wonderfully delicious. And he still had enough to stretch out the luxury for a week or more.

Then it had been time to drill with the regulars. Even though they had defeated the Creeks, General Jackson said it was only one battle in the war. They had to stay sharp and ready. Their countrymen were counting on them.

"Are you asleep, boy?" The captain's voice prodded him forward.

Asher shook his head. Apparently thinking about Rebekah

had led him to daydreaming as he teased her about doing. He saluted and hurried to the tent into which the Indian chief had disappeared earlier. He pulled back the flap, surprised at the tableau in front of him. Maps had been rolled and stacked in one corner. Neither of the guards was inside, but several high-ranking officers were present, most of whom he recognized. He nodded to Lieutenant John Ross, who sat next to General Jackson, a quill poised in his hand as though he was ready to pen whatever words his commander might utter. Jackson was talking and nodding at the Indian whom Asher would have thought would be kneeling at Old Hickory's feet instead of being treated like an honored guest.

As he snapped a salute, Asher couldn't help but notice several similarities between the general and the Indian chief. They were of comparable height and age and shared intense blue eyes that seemed to see right through a man's skin to his soul. While General Jackson's distinctive mane contrasted with the darker hair of the stranger, there was something about them—some attitude or stance—that made them appear more like distant cousins than deadly adversaries.

Both men bore the scars of many battles, but those scars only enhanced their charismatic appeal. Even though the general had undoubtedly lost weight during the six months since they'd left Nashville, no one could say he had lost an ounce of his steely determination. It was that strength of will coupled with his genuine concern for his men that had won the love and admiration of both volunteer and regular soldiers.

"Soldier, I want you to meet a man who has seen the inevitability of defeat and decided to act with honor. This is William Weatherford, formerly known as Chief Red Eagle."

Asher controlled his features with some difficulty. What was going on here? Why did General Jackson call his enemy an honorable man?

"Thank you, sir." He turned to the stranger. "Mr. Weatherford." Asher observed the man's eyes narrow as he and Weatherford studied each other.

With an abrupt nod, Weatherford returned his attention to Jackson. A wordless message seemed to pass between the two.

"Mr. Landon, your commendable loyalty and devotion to duty have been many times brought to my attention. So I have a special assignment to offer you. Mr. Weatherford, here, needs an escort out of the area. He has expressed his willingness to work toward the absolute and peaceful surrender of any holdouts there may be among the Creek nation. You will accompany him for the next two months before returning here to report the success or failure of his efforts."

General Jackson turned back to Weatherford. "And if any harm comes to this man, or if you should change your mind and decide to once again take up arms against this sovereign nation, your life will be forfeit. Do we understand each other?"

Weatherford nodded. He was obviously a man of few words.

"You'll leave at daybreak." General Jackson nodded in his direction, and Asher thought for a moment he saw a smile of encouragement. "Dismissed."

two

As Rebekah and her pa drew closer to Nashville, they began to see homesteads here and there, as well as other travelers. They topped a hill, and the city lay before them as if it had sprung from the banks of the river that twisted through it.

Even though she'd traveled to Nashville before, Rebekah was amazed at the beehive of activity. Carriages, horses, and pedestrians filled every street. On the main thoroughfare, dozens of people scurried along as if they were on important errands. She wrinkled her nose at the multitude of smells. An unpleasant odor of hot iron and horse leavings emanated from the livery stable they passed. But a little farther down the street, the smell of fresh bread made her want to stop and visit the bakery.

They passed a millinery, its windows filled with hats ranging from simple bonnets to wide-brimmed, feathered concoctions that looked much too heavy to wear. "How will you ever find Aunt Dolly's home?" Rebekah's head was spinning with the hustle and bustle around them.

"See the mercantile?" Pa pointed at a two-story building on his left. "You need to go one block past it and then turn down the next street to the right."

"There it is." She clapped her hands, excited to have recognized the tall windows and portico of Dolly Quinn's three-story brick home. Then her spirits plunged. "Everything is so different from home."

"You'll be fine, honey." He winked at her and drew back on Bessie's reins, bringing the wagon to a halt. A young boy ran up and offered to hold the horse. Pa hesitated only a moment before nodding. Then he climbed down and helped her alight from the hard seat.

Rebekah pushed the folds of her cloak back and shifted her weight from one foot to another as she waited for someone to open the front door in response to her pa's knock.

The door creaked on its hinges, revealing a shocking sight. Gone was Aunt Dolly's elegantly appointed entry hall. Family portraits hung askew, and a mop leaned against one wall. The rug was bunched haphazardly under a window. Dust could be seen on every surface, from the floor to the furniture to the windows. She even spied a cobweb swaying gently in one corner of the hall. "Oh, my. I believe Aunt Dolly does need my help."

The black woman who had opened the door looked as rumpled as the rug behind her. There were dark circles under her eyes, her cap was askew, and her apron was covered with stains. "Oh, thank the Lord you're here, Mr. William."

"Hello. . .Harriet, isn't it?" Pa had the oddest expression on his face. Like he wanted to run away from the chaos inside Aunt Dolly's house.

For a brief moment, Rebekah wanted to run away, too. Could she take care of her aunt and see to the house at the same time?

Harriet curtsied and waved them inside. "I know it looks bad, but since Maude moved with her husband to Knoxville and left me with all the work, I'm a little behind. Now that you and your daughter are here, I'm sure we can get everything back in order."

Rebekah followed Harriet toward the parlor, her eyes taking in the general air of neglect. But after the first shock, she realized things weren't as bad as they initially appeared to be. With a bucket of water and some rags, this room could look pristine in an afternoon. The thought gave her courage.

She turned to reassure her father and realized he was still

in the hallway. "Pa?"

"I'd better get your stuff from the wagon."

Harriet reached back to untie the strings of her apron. "I can help."

"No, no. There's not much to unload. You take Rebekah upstairs to see her aunt. Tell Dolly I'll be up in a minute to visit with her before I go back home."

Harriet's smile was a broad, white slash that eased the worry from her face. She nodded and led the way upstairs. "It's good that you're here. Your aunt will rest easier and recover her health faster."

Rebekah followed her reluctantly. She would much prefer to stay on the first floor and delay seeing her ailing aunt. It would be hard to see a loved one so weak. But that was the reason she was here, so she raised her chin and stiffened her resolve. Everyone was counting on her—she would not let them down.

Harriet opened Aunt Dolly's door and led the way into a seemingly cavernous room. Draperies covered every window, leaving the bedchamber dark and gloomy even at midday. A large rice bed stood in the center of the room, its tall, thin posts drawing Rebekah's gaze upward to the ornate carvings on the ceiling. Anyone lying down could spend hours looking at the fascinating patterns above.

A series of hacking coughs indicated her aunt's presence in the large bed. "What is it? Who's there?"

"It's me, and look who has arrived." Harriet plumped a pillow and helped Dolly to a sitting position. "It's your niece, Miss Rebekah. And Mr. William will be up after unloading her things."

Another fit of coughing ensued, and Rebekah wondered what to do.

"Come. . .closer. . .child." Each word was punctuated by another cough.

"Don't speak, Aunt Dolly. You need to rest." She bent over and placed a quick peck on the older woman's cheek.

"That's right." Harriet added her support as she smoothed the quilt covering Aunt Dolly. "You're going to get better soon now. Just you wait and see."

Rebekah sent up a fervent prayer that Harriet's words would come true and, after a quick glance around, that God would give her strength to tackle all that lay ahead.

⁂

Rebekah ran loving fingers across the oak dining table. Her brown eyes stared back at her from its rich surface. She noticed a spot of dirt on her nose and rubbed at it impatiently, turning it into a streak. Her wheat-colored hair, drawn back with a ribbon, had pulled loose from its binding. It would be nice to cut it short like a boy's instead of having to deal with the tangles. But Asher might not like that. If Asher ever returned.

She looked around the room, satisfied with its appearance. After several weeks, Aunt Dolly's house sparkled with cleanliness. She had interviewed and engaged another maid, making it possible to get caught up with all of the household tasks. But the greatest blessing of all was Aunt Dolly's returning health. Her chronic cough had finally yielded to the broths and teas Rebekah and Harriet had concocted, as well as to the many prayers they sent heavenward. Rebekah knew that had been the true cure.

A knock on the front door interrupted her musings. Rebekah was glad to hear it. While Aunt Dolly was not fully recovered, she was able to come downstairs and have short visits with the guests who came by to check on her. Seeing her friends always seemed to cheer her up.

From the dining room, Rebekah could not see who was at the front door, but she could hear Harriet's booming tones and a feminine voice answering. After a minute, she heard

Harriet climbing the stairs to fetch Aunt Dolly.

Rebekah decided she'd stay hidden in the dining room as long as possible. She didn't want anyone to see her with her hair all messed up. It was hard enough making conversation with strangers when she was tidy. The time passed slowly while she waited. When she judged it safe, she slipped out of the room. . .and ran into Aunt Dolly and her guest in the hallway.

"Oh, good. There you are." Her aunt put a hand on Rebekah's arm and turned to the dark-haired woman next to her. "I have someone you'll enjoy meeting, Rachel. This is my sister's oldest daughter, Rebekah. Rebekah," she continued, "this is Rachel Jackson, the wife of our illustrious military commander, General Andrew Jackson."

Rebekah could not believe her ears. She'd expected a famous personage like Andrew Jackson to be married to a stunning beauty—not a short, matronly woman dressed in a plain calico dress. She looked like she'd be at home on Pa's farm.

"I've heard good things about you, my dear."

Rebekah blushed. She didn't deserve any praise, given her unchristian attention to Mrs. Jackson's looks rather than her heart. She bobbed a quick curtsy, her eyes on the floor. She hoped God would forgive her for her earlier thoughts.

"She's a wonderful help." Aunt Dolly patted her arm. "Not only does she supervise Harriet and the maids, but she also reads and sings to me, and she has even prepared several medicaments that have made my recovery possible."

Rebekah's cheeks grew even hotter as the praise continued. She was so unworthy. She'd not known how to do much of anything when she arrived. Harriet knew more about running the household than Rebekah. She'd have been overwhelmed without any help.

"Rebekah." Dolly's tone sounded different, like she had a

wonderful secret to impart. "I mentioned your young man to Mrs. Jackson. She hears from Andrew quite regularly, so she's going to ask him for a report on Asher. Won't that be lovely?"

Rebekah's heart stuttered. She looked toward Rachel. "C–Could you?"

"I'd love to do that for you, Rebekah. I know how worried you must be." She patted Rebekah's hot cheek. "I'm certain he's fine, but we all know how men sometimes don't have a mind to do as they ought."

"Thank you so much. I'll be forever in your debt." Tears pricked at the edges of Rebekah's eyes.

"It's not any trouble." Rachel turned back to Dolly. "I'll let you know as soon as I hear something."

Rebekah sent a quick prayer upward that Rachel would hear good news and hear it very soon.

three

"I insist, my dear." Aunt Dolly's voice gained a slight edge.

Six months of living in her aunt's home had taught Rebekah that it was best to acquiesce when that raspy edge appeared. Failure to do so could result in a relapse or a fainting spell. Once, her aunt had been so distraught, that she had taken to her bed for a week, refusing to eat or allow anyone to visit her.

Rebekah nodded and took the dress her aunt proffered. "You're too generous, Aunt Dolly."

"Now, now. Do remember to call me Dolly. There is no reason to remind others of my advancing age."

Rebekah smiled. "No one would think you're a day over twenty, Au—Dolly. You are full of energy now that you've recovered your health. And your complexion. How do you keep it so clear and smooth? I'm always fighting freckles."

Dolly sighed and patted her cheek. "You're such a sweet thing. I don't know how I ever managed without you here." She shooed Rebekah toward the door. "Go on. You must try on the dress. I have the feeling we'll need to make some alterations."

Rebekah hurried down the wide hall to her bedroom, which never failed to cheer her with its pink beribboned drapes and four-poster bed. The canopy that topped it made the bed seem like her special refuge. Double doors on the far wall opened out onto a small balcony overlooking the street. When she'd first arrived, the noise from the street often woke her at night, but now she was used to it.

She laid the dress on her bed, its pale yellow fabric reminding her of spring daisies in the meadow back home.

She sighed. It was not that she was unhappy staying with Aunt Dolly...no...Dolly. She really needed to remember not to call her *Aunt*. Even though her father had come to check on them a couple of times, she missed her family. She hadn't seen her mother and siblings since spring. Little Donny was probably through teething, and there was no telling how much Eleanor had grown between March and June. Rebekah knew this was a busy time on the farm. She wondered how well they were getting along without her help.

A wave of homesickness swept over her, but Rebekah refused to give in to the melancholy. She had much too much to be thankful for. Including the gorgeous dress lying on her bed. Used to homemade dresses woven from cotton or wool and often handed down from her ma, Rebekah had never owned anything half so beautiful. Her fingers traced the delicate lace outlining the neck and sleeves of the dress. The bodice was high, accentuated by a golden length of ribbon that would fall gracefully toward the wearer's ankles after it was tied in the back. The skirt was quite narrow and looked too revealing to Rebekah's eyes. There was not much room to wear petticoats or pantaloons beneath the dress. It would almost certainly reveal a lady's limbs if she had need to hurry across a room. She was sure it was the latest fashion and just as sure Pa would frown on her wearing it.

What would Asher think if he saw her in such attire? Would his eyes light up with admiration, or would he be shocked? Her eyes closed as she imagined the scene. A dress like this would be worn for a fancy party. Asher would be wearing formal clothes, his thick chestnut hair falling just so against his brow. His broad shoulders and proud bearing would be shown off to advantage in his evening dress, and his boots would gleam in the candlelight as he walked across the room to greet her. All of the other ladies in the room would follow his progress with hope, and they would be filled with envy when he stopped at her side. He would bow, and she would curtsy. And he would take her hand in his, maybe even press a kiss against it in the European manner. . . .

Her aunt fluttered into the bedroom, ending her daydream. "Whatever are you doing, Rebekah? Are you not anxious to see how the gown looks?"

"I'm sorry, Dolly. I was—"

"I know. You were daydreaming again. Really, you have got to rid yourself of that habit. What if you were attacked by a bear or Indians?" Dolly paused and shivered. "When you begin daydreaming, you lose any awareness of your surroundings. You would not recognize the danger until it was too late."

Rebekah hung her head in shame. It was true. She did spend too much time imagining the future. It would be better to spend her time dealing with the present.

A knock at the bedroom door interrupted the women, and they turned to see Harriet peeking at them. "Excuse me, ma'am. You have a guest."

Dolly brushed the skirt of her day dress, smoothing the blue material with practiced fingers. "Who is it?"

"Mrs. Jackson."

"Oh, my." Dolly clapped her hands and turned to Rebekah. "Perhaps we should leave the dress for now. We'll adjust it later. Let's go find out what news Rachel has of the fighting."

Rebekah wanted to leap over her aunt to get downstairs and hear the news, but she forced herself to take her time and mimic Dolly's tiny steps. Her aunt always appeared to float into a room, a technique Rebekah would like to acquire so she could impress Asher once he returned home. Wouldn't he be surprised at her cosmopolitan polish when she approached him, resplendent in her new yellow dress?

"Good morning, Rachel," Dolly's warm tones welcomed her friend.

Rachel's smile was wide, transforming her face from plain

to angelic. Her expression was a reflection of her disposition—gentle and sweet. There might be some in Nashville who would condemn her for her past, but not Rebekah or Dolly. Rebekah didn't understand the complaint people made against Rachel and Andrew Jackson. Something about Rachel having been married before.

The two older ladies chitchatted about the weather and the latest Indian sighting while they waited for Harriet to serve refreshments.

Rebekah had learned many rules that were observed in the city, but today she could have cried with frustration as they exchanged social niceties. She would have much preferred the country way of going straight to the point. Clenching her teeth, Rebekah balanced on the edge of Dolly's settee and picked up the embroidery she had been working on for the past week. It would give her hands something to do besides twist themselves into a knot.

Harriet brought in the silver service, and Dolly handed round, delicate china cups filled with tea. Rachel helped herself to one of the maple cookies that were piled on a china plate, but Rebekah shook her head. There was no way she could choke anything down right now. Not until she knew the reason for Mrs. Jackson's unannounced visit.

"I have very important news, ladies. And I knew you would want to learn of it as soon as possible."

Dolly dismissed Harriet with a nod. "Whatever can it be?"

"Ouch." Rebekah jerked her thumb from the needle that had pierced it, dropped her handwork, and quickly wrapped a handkerchief around the tiny wound.

Dolly and Rachel looked toward her.

"I'm all right. I'm just anxious. *Please* go ahead and tell us your news."

Rachel opened her reticule and pulled a sheet of stationery from it. "Andrew has sent for me to join him in New Orleans at the beginning of the year. And I want the two of you to travel with me."

Rebekah squealed, then caught herself and coughed. She would get to see Asher! She could wear the yellow dress! She could almost hear his voice greeting her, his surprise overtaken with joy as they were reunited. Oh, how romantic! Her mind's eye revised the scene she had created earlier, putting Asher in his dashing uniform instead of evening wear.

Aunt Dolly was saying something about plans and dangers, but Rebekah pushed those aside. She had six long weeks in which to convince her aunt and her parents that she should go. She wanted to hug Rachel Jackson, who was beaming at both of them. She would allow absolutely nothing to prevent her from making this trip. If the men could not return to Nashville, why shouldn't their ladies go to them?

❧

Asher strode under the graceful, wrought facades supported by cast-iron columns. This part of New Orleans had been carefully laid out, its streets forming squares within squares. He had to admit that the uniformity of its design made the area very easy to navigate. Much easier than navigating the political situation of the city.

He had nothing but the greatest admiration for General Jackson, even though he might not agree with every decision the man made. Like trusting the Baratarian pirates. There was no telling if they wouldn't decide to switch sides in the middle of the looming battle.

His musings were interrupted by a feminine scream that seemed to issue from within a knot of soldiers ahead of him. Putting a hand on his pistol, Asher quickened his pace. "What's going on here?"

A man he didn't recognize answered the question. "We wasn't doing nothin'."

"Stand aside. I distinctly heard a lady."

"Oh, please, kind sir. Save me from these ruffians. They've trapped me."

Asher's anger soared. How dare they accost a woman in the streets in broad daylight? "You should be ashamed of yourselves." He drew himself to his full height and met each man's gaze separately. Only one of them seemed disposed to challenge Asher's authority, but one of his buddies pulled on his arm, and they all drifted away.

Once they had disappeared around the corner, Asher turned his attention to the young woman he had rescued. She was slender, with hair as dark as coal. From her expensive clothing, he guessed she was from a wealthy family. "Where is your attendant?"

She looked up at him, her brows drawn together over eyes that shone like glass. She was so frightened he could see her shoulders shaking. "I shouldn't have come alone. It's just that my slave, Jemma, has yellow fever. And the day was so pretty. I thought I would walk to the *Place d'Armes* and watch the soldiers march. I didn't think it would be. . .dangerous."

Asher let his frown deepen. The girl had probably learned her lesson, but he would not condone her actions. He shivered to think of Rebekah doing anything so precipitous. But that was foolish, as his Rebekah was a model of modest behavior. She would never go out alone in a big city, especially not on the eve of battle.

"Where do you live, Miss. . ."

"Lewis. I'm Alexandra Lewis. Papa is part of the militia. My mama and I came down to visit with him. Our rooms are only a block away. I can—"

"No, you cannot. As your papa is fighting with General Jackson, I consider it my duty to see that you are returned safely to the bosom of your family." He held out his arm, annoyed when she hesitated. Did she think he would rescue her from a mob only to attack her himself? "Allow me to introduce myself. Asher Landon, at your service."

When she laid her hand on his arm, he could feel it shivering even though the temperature was quite warm for a December afternoon. Immediately his conscience smote him. Alexandra Lewis was clearly still overcome by the attentions of those men. Not surprising for a young lady of such obvious gentility. He patted her hand and gave her an encouraging smile. She had nothing to fear from him.

His reassurance must have been effective. They had hardly walked a full block before she began talking to him as if they were old friends. Her exuberance reminded him of Rebekah.

"Are you going to the Richelieus' ball, Mr. Landon?"

"If we're not battling the British." As an officer, he was expected to attend. The general thought it was good policy to socialize with the local gentry.

"Papa is taking Mama and me. But I'm so worried no one will dance with me."

"I doubt a pretty girl like you will have to worry about that. The men will likely line up for the honor."

"But what about you, Mr. Landon? Would you dance with me?"

Asher frowned. Miss Lewis was somewhat forward, but maybe it was only a bit of naïveté. With his experience in the military, perhaps he should take her under his wing and protect her a bit.

"I would be honored, Miss Lewis."

❧

Rebekah wrapped her arms tighter against her waist, burrowing into the layers of her cloak for comfort. A damp, gray mist wound its way around tree trunks as the muddy Mississippi River swept their flat-bottomed boat southward toward their destination. Rachel and Dolly had already retired for the evening to their shared cabin, but Rebekah was not sleepy.

What would this year bring? Last year, she'd wondered the

same thing. And she'd been filled with the same optimism that currently kept her from seeking sleep. If someone had told her that she would go another whole year without Asher, she'd have refused to accept the possibility.

But that was exactly what had happened. She had marked his anniversary date with abiding hope, knowing that he would soon be released from service. But he had not appeared. Then in the spring when other men returned from the war, faces hardened and gaunt from their experiences, she'd awaited his return patiently. She'd been ready to nurse him back to excellent health with kind Christian concern and loving care.

Still no Asher.

Then the victory over the Indians had been reported in Nashville, and she had waited to welcome her returning hero. She'd sewn a sampler to commemorate the date and the valorous deeds of the Tennessee militia. Many was the night she'd knelt by her bed and prayed earnestly for his safe return.

Her spirits had dipped to a new low when it became apparent he would remain with General Jackson. Finally, *finally*, her opportunity had arrived the day Rachel Jackson burst in on her and her aunt with her marvelous, daring proposal.

So here she stood gazing at the sky and trying to imagine what her family was doing. She'd missed getting to see them at Christmas, but that was a sacrifice she'd been willing to make as she and Aunt Dolly prepared for their trip. The desire to return home paled in comparison to her desire to see Asher.

It had taken several letters from Mrs. Jackson and Aunt Dolly to convince her parents that Rebekah should accompany them on their trip. They had finally yielded, unable to withstand Dolly's assurances that their daughter would be safeguarded and her pleas to them to remember how they had felt when they were courting.

A creaking board alerted her to someone's presence on deck. She smiled at her new friend. Despite the disparity in age, she had grown very close to Rachel Jackson during their trip.

"Isn't it time for you to come inside?" Rachel's skirt billowed gently in the humid evening breeze. "I have already sent my son to bed, and Dolly and I are about to retire. We don't like leaving you out here alone."

"I get more excited with every day. How long do you think it will be before we get to New Orleans?"

"The captain said we'll get to Natchez tomorrow. Then he'll need to drop off some of his cargo and load new provisions for the last leg of our journey. We'll likely be there within the week."

"I cannot wait."

The two women stood side by side for several minutes, watching the dark water swirl around the edges of the boat. Then the older woman put an arm around Rebekah's shoulders and hugged her tightly. "Me, either."

four

"Victory!" The whole world seemed to breathe it. General Jackson had done it! He had routed the British against all odds. Rebekah felt like a part of the triumph as her friend, Rachel, fairly beamed her happiness and pride in the accomplishments of her husband. He was a real American hero. Everyone agreed the battle had been instrumental in proving to the world that Americans would not be defeated. Nearly every plantation they passed sent heartfelt messages of thanks and praise to be delivered to General Jackson. And now they had arrived in New Orleans, eager to end their journey and join the celebration.

Rebekah picked every step with great care. She didn't want to end up falling off the debris-strewn wharf into the muddy currents below. Was it always so dirty here? In Natchez, the wooden platform used for loading and unloading goods and passengers had been freshly swept and its planks uniformly spaced and flat. Here the gaps between boards looked huge, and some of them were splintered and lying at odd angles. She had avoided one that looked too rotten to hold the weight of a baby, much less one of the tired passengers.

She reached for Aunt Dolly's hand when they came to a spot where the barricade had been removed so they might enter the town. Her nose wrinkled at the sight before them. The streets were mud-choked, rutted canals that grabbed at horses' hooves and the wheels of the carts they dragged. Thank goodness there were raised walkways for people, but what Rebekah could see of them showed them to be barely cleaner or in better repair than the wharf.

"This way, ladies." Neither Rachel nor her adopted son, Andrew, seemed perturbed by the mayhem or the general state of decay around them. She waved a hand toward an open carriage.

"However did you secure such an excellent conveyance?" Dolly smiled at the ebony-faced driver who offered her a helping hand. "I was sure we would have to walk or at best ride in the back of a wagon."

Rebekah waited for Dolly to pull in her skirts somewhat before settling herself next to her aunt, their backs to the driver's seat. Rachel smiled widely as she and her son took the seats on the opposite side of the carriage. "The boat captain arranged it. He apparently told someone that the hero's family had arrived."

The driver closed the door and clambered nimbly onto his wooden seat. He said something to the horse, but Rebekah could not understand his words.

"What language is he speaking?"

"In his last letter, Andrew told me that the inhabitants here speak more French than English. It makes sense when you think about it. France, through her Acadian settlers, built the town."

"Humph." Dolly raised her brows. "I've heard French all my life, but I didn't understand him any better than Rebekah. It must be some local dialect."

Rebekah nodded her head and looked around at the people they were passing. Everyone seemed excited, if a little forward for her taste. Strangers waved at them—men in rough buckskins reminiscent of home, as well as uniformed men who made her ache to see Asher.

A loud noise made all four of the occupants turn their heads. Telltale wisps of smoke trailed from a raised pistol. Had the man killed someone or just shot into the air? His dark face looked dangerous, and Rebekah noticed that the stranger wore gold jewelry around his neck like a woman. Her breath caught when their eyes met. He smiled, and her heartbeat accelerated. What a handsome—

"Rebekah." Aunt Dolly's voice was sharp in her ear. "Do not look at him."

She jerked her head away and focused on her hands in her lap.

"Don't be too hard on the girl." Rachel's voice was choked with laughter. "He was a charmer, and I doubt we'll see him again."

"Still, she must be aware of the dangers. You or I might not always be around to protect her."

"True, but I can understand her curiosity."

Several minutes passed before Rebekah dared to raise her gaze, and by then, the bold stranger had been left behind. As they got farther from the waterfront, the townspeople seemed even odder. She was beginning to see more women strolling along the walkways, but her mouth dropped open when she realized that several were allowing men to clasp them around their waists. Some were even kissing men! Right out on the street!

Would Asher expect her to allow him that freedom in this debauched setting? Well, he had better not. She had been raised properly, and he would have to respect that. But maybe she would allow him to hug her. A blush heated her cheeks at the thought. It had been more than a year since they'd seen each other. Surely she could allow him to show some delight at their reunion with a brief hug.

It would be so different from the last time. She wouldn't be distraught, and he wouldn't be trying to comfort her. No, this time it would be completely romantic. She could almost feel his arms around her waist, hear his heart beating against her cheek. . . .

The carriage stopped, and the pleasant thoughts ended. "Is this our hotel?" Rebekah asked.

The building was at least three stories high, but it leaned somewhat to the right, as though it had been wounded in the recent battle. Tantalizing odors of spicy meat and stews, however, emanated from somewhere nearby. She squared her shoulders. It would not be so bad. And it was worth it to see her beloved Asher.

The women disembarked and entered the shadowy front room of the hotel. The innkeeper was a short man with a bald head and round stomach, who bowed over and over again while wishing them a "*bonju.*" Even with her limited French, Rebekah knew the word was *bonjour*, but she smiled and waited behind the older women as they arranged for a suite of rooms and to have an early dinner brought up.

Her gaze wandered to the dining room, where a more sedate group of citizens sat at long wooden tables to eat and converse. She could tell from their dress that they were higher class, but still, they were unlike any other people she'd ever met in her life. Their voices drifted out of the room, the words melodic if incomprehensible.

A new couple entered from the street, and she could not tear her gaze away. The woman was stunning—tall and graceful with the most beautiful skin she'd ever seen stretched across high cheekbones. She had a generous mouth and dark eyes that hinted at exotic mysteries. The woman laughed at something the gentleman said, and they entered the dining room, greeting the other diners and being hailed in return.

"Come along."

Her aunt's words snagged Rebekah's attention, and she followed her aunt to the room they would share, while Rachel and her son retired to the adjoining room.

Dolly and Rebekah hardly stopped for the next hour, getting their trunks emptied and instructing the chambermaids as to the placement and care of their clothing. Between commands, her aunt continually bemoaned having left Harriet at home.

Rebekah was too glad to be off the river and finally in New Orleans to quibble about who helped them unpack. She lovingly pulled out a cloth-wrapped bundle and placed it on the table next to her Bible.

The sounds of drums and marching feet caught her attention, and Rebekah flew to the window facing the street that had brought them to the hotel. Pushing open the wooden shutter, she gazed at the street, now turning orange under the rays of the setting sun.

As Dolly joined her at the window, a battalion turned the corner and marched with rough precision down the street. Their uniforms were streaked with dirt and mud, but their faces smiled as the onlookers cheered and clapped.

"Do you see him?" her aunt asked.

After frantically searching the men's faces, Rebekah sighed her disappointment. "No, I don't think so." Still, they watched until the battalion disappeared from view.

Aunt Dolly leaned forward and pulled the shutter closed. "Even though it's not as cold here as at home, I imagine the air will be quite cool tonight."

Rebekah nodded and turned away from the window. "Would you like to see the gift I have for Asher?"

She looked toward the older woman, who frowned. "Do you think it's seemly for you to give him a gift? You are not betrothed after all."

Rebekah grabbed the cloth bundle and held it to her chest. "It's only a handkerchief with his initials stitched on it. Remember when you had the parlor draperies replaced at home?"

Dolly nodded.

"The old linings still had some wear left, so I used them to make scarves and things. I even used some squares on the back side of the quilt we were working on."

"How practical of you, dear, but there is plenty of nice cloth stored away at home." Dolly patted her on the shoulder. "I sometimes forget that you were raised without the luxuries I take for granted. I suppose it will be acceptable for you to give the handkerchief to Asher. We will call it a congratulatory gift because of the victory."

Rebekah breathed a sigh of relief at her aunt's decision. She wanted to see Asher open her gift. Would his long fingers trace the outline of his initials? Initials that her very hands had stitched. And then would he place it in an inner pocket next to his heart? She sighed again. It would be perfect. She could hardly wait.

A knock on the door that separated their room from Rachel's room signaled that dinner was ready. Before joining her companions for dinner, Rebekah took a moment to carefully tuck the white cloth into the top drawer of her bureau.

"Your aunt and I have had the most inspired idea," Rachel greeted her as she took her place at the table. "I have discovered that there is going to be a victory ball at the Beaumonts' tomorrow evening. I will be expected to arrive in time to partake of the dinner with my husband, but what if we surprise your young man by allowing you and Dolly to appear unannounced in the middle of the ball?"

Rebekah's breath caught, and she could not stop herself from smiling. Perhaps she would finally be reunited with her love tomorrow.

five

Asher straightened the cuff on his uniform and turned to face the window. The setting sun cast enough light on the pane to allow him to see his reflection. He practiced a smile and straightened his neckcloth. It wouldn't do to appear slovenly at the victory celebration.

His smile widened. The politicians in Washington would have to give General Jackson his due now that he had soundly whipped the British forces. There was no doubt America owed her freedom to the intelligence and perseverance of one man. Asher was thrilled to have played a small part in the exciting events.

His smile dimmed a bit in the windowpane. There was only one small wisp of disappointment in his life these days. He missed his home. He closed his eyes and imagined his parents' house, the walk swept clean of winter snow, a roaring fire in the parlor. He could almost taste his ma's apple pie.

And Rebekah would be there, too, with her sparkling brown eyes and worshipful smile. How he ached to talk with her. No one understood him better than Rebekah.

He wanted to tell her about the friends he had made—white men, Indians, and French Acadians. He had been promoted several times and now held the rank of captain. And surely he would move even higher as his career followed General Jackson's. Why, by the time he got home to Rebekah and his parents, he might even be a colonel. How surprised and proud they would be.

Rebekah would forgive him for postponing their future when she realized how much his decision to remain with the militia for the past year would benefit them. His pay would provide a nice home for them, while his connections would give them entrée into the finest circles of Nashville society. His Rebekah would be the best hostess in the whole country—charming, sweet, and talented. Together, they would make a name for themselves. There was no telling what all they would attain once peace had been declared.

Asher nodded at his reflection and drew a deep breath. He swept his palm across the hair that tended to fall down over his forehead, only to feel it fall forward once again. With a grunt, he strode to the tall bureau that stood on the far side of his bed and grabbed the pomade. As he returned to the window, someone knocked at his door.

"Time to leave!"

Asher subdued the lock of hair and turned to the door, joining the other young officers who were making their way down the stairs and across the French Quarter. They walked up St. Ann Street to the two-story mansion where the ball was being held.

Their arrival caused a bit of a stir as the society dames whispered behind their fans. He was reminded of the chicken yard back home. The older women were the laying hens, full of clucking and posturing to attract the attention of the rooster. The more timid "hatchlings" peeked over their chaperones' shoulders but quickly hid their dark glances from the interested gazes of the soldiers.

Asher leaned against a column and watched the scene unfold before him. His ears were tickled by the accents as the guests mingled together. Several couples danced to the strains of a minuet, while dozens of people stood around talking. The parties he had attended with his parents in Nashville were as dull as a rusty saber in comparison to this glittering ensemble.

"That's him, Papa. He's the one I told you about—the one

who rescued me that afternoon." Asher turned to see the young lady whom he had found wandering the Quarter two weeks earlier. Amazing that they would run into each other so quickly in the press of guests.

A heavy hand slapped the gold braiding on his shoulder. He turned to face a short man with a gray fringe of hair and mustache to match.

"I'm Colonel James Lewis, Captain. And I'm pleased to finally get to say thank you for the mighty fine thing you did."

Asher shook the man's hand and introduced himself, noting the colonel's navy blue uniform with wide lapels and an impressive number of colorful medals. He wondered if Colonel Lewis was a seasoned soldier or a politician who had only recently donned his uniform. Either way, it had taken all of them to route the British.

A slight movement brought his attention back to the pretty girl standing to the right of the colonel. "It is my hope that you will formally introduce me to the lovely lady, sir."

"Of course it is." The colonel puffed out his chest. "All the young men want to meet my daughter."

Asher was again reminded of the chicken yard, this time of the strutting pride of a rooster.

"Captain Landon, I would like you to meet my daughter, Alexandra Lewis." He drew her forward. "Alexandra, Captain Asher Landon."

Asher bowed and reached for her hand, holding it gently as he kissed the air some two inches above her elbow-length glove.

"Captain Landon, thank you so much for saving me that day. I have told Mama and Papa that I would surely have perished if not for your gallantry."

Asher straightened and patted her hand. "You exaggerate, Miss Lewis. I did nothing more than any other gentleman would do when in the same circumstances."

"I beg to differ." Colonel Lewis reached into the breast pocket of his coat and withdrew a square of white. "Here is my card. Come see me at the general's headquarters in a few days. I believe I may have use for a young man whose heart is in the right place."

"Thank you, sir. It will be my pleasure."

"Yes, good. But for now, you young people enjoy yourselves." He shooed his daughter in Asher's general direction.

Asher held his hand out to her. "If you would be so kind. . ."

Alexandra put her hand in his, and he thought it trembled slightly.

He smiled to alleviate her discomfort. It was easy to understand why such a young miss should feel a little overwhelmed. "It is good to see you recovered from your. . ." He hesitated, searching for the right word.

"Stupidity." Alexandra's gaze dropped toward the slender skirt of her gown.

Asher stood opposite her on the dance floor, wondering how to alleviate her embarrassment without condoning her behavior that afternoon. Of course, it wasn't his place to chastise Alexandra, but he thought how he would like for his younger sister, Mary, to be treated in a similar situation. Or Rebekah. But what foolishness. Even though Rebekah and Alexandra were probably about the same age, his Rebekah would never be so imprudent as to wander city streets alone. What would she say to Alexandra? She would be gracious and kind, of course.

"I was going to say 'adventure.'" He was rewarded when her sparkling gaze swept upward to meet his. It felt good to know he was responsible for the tentative smile that curved her lips. Rebekah would be proud of him for easing Alexandra's discomfort. He bowed to her curtsy as required by the French contra dance and concentrated on presenting a polished appearance on the dance floor.

The gossamer material of Alexandra's rose gown swept his legs as they turned in unison. He placed a hand on her waist and stepped forward, then took two steps back. They faced each other again. "I cannot believe how many people have come tonight."

"Yes, and they are still arriving."

Asher followed the direction of her gaze. A press of people stood at the top of the staircase. He wondered if the ballroom would be able to hold all of them.

⁂

Candles lit every corner of the ballroom, their light reflected on the mirrored walls. Rebekah's eyes drank in the sight of the graceful dancers. The twirling dresses of the ladies looked like a multihued rose garden swaying in a gentle wind. Even the men on the dance floor were colorful. Some wore evening dress—long coats and starched white shirts—but many were in uniforms from the different battalions who had come together to fight under General Jackson's leadership. Some of the uniforms were green, some blue, and she even saw one man in a white uniform. It was nearly more than she could comprehend as she descended the grand staircase with Aunt Dolly.

The musicians ended their song as she reached the bottom of the staircase, and she saw Asher standing tall and handsome in his uniform. Her Asher. The man who loved her. How blessed she was to hold his affection. Happiness, pride, excitement, and anticipation all burst open inside her like fireworks in the nighttime sky.

Rebekah moved toward him as if drawn by an unseen hand. It might not be seemly, but she wanted to feel his embrace. She looked for the same feelings to be mirrored in his expression, but instead she saw confusion on his handsome face.

"Asher?" She stopped a few feet short of him, suddenly uncertain of herself, of him, of reality. Instead of rushing toward her in excitement and wonder, he was still standing in the same place.

And who was the woman standing right next to him? She was everything Rebekah was not—tall, poised, and exotically beautiful. She looked very womanly and very certain of herself. Her hair sparkled like polished mahogany in the glow of the candles. Her pink ball gown was cut low across her chest, showing far too much skin to be considered respectable back home in Nashville.

Rebekah could not believe how she had fretted over the fit of her own gown. It was about as revealing as a flour sack when compared to the straight skirts of the other woman's gown. Why the dress was so short, she imagined that the other woman's *ankles* could be seen if she dared to dance. Did Asher now find that sort of woman attractive?

Her gaze searched his face. Was he even the same person she'd fallen in love with? He looked so different. His face was tanned from exposure to the Southern sun, and his shoulders looked twice as wide as they'd been the last time she saw him. That day at the farm might as well have been more than a decade ago rather than a little over a year.

Rebekah drew a deep breath. "Excuse me. I. . .I thought you were s—someone I knew." She turned on her heel and pushed her way through the crowd. She refused to let him see how he'd torn her heart in two.

"Rebekah! Rebekah, come back."

She heard his voice, but she could not turn back. After all of her dreams and expectations, she wanted nothing more than to leave. She wanted to leave this house, this town, this foreign world, and travel back to a place and time where everything had been right.

Her blurry vision led her into the wide hallway. To her left, incoming guests crowded the entryway, so Rebekah turned right. She had only gotten a dozen paces away from the ballroom when a hand clamped itself onto her shoulder.

"Rebekah." It was Asher's voice. He spun her around and pulled her shoulders against him.

Rebekah felt like the rag doll she'd played with as a child—floppy with no backbone. Hot tears burned her eyes and trickled down her cheeks. She could feel one of his hands patting her on the back, while the other smoothed the material at her shoulder. After a few minutes the tears slowed, then ceased entirely. The crushing disappointment was still there, but it had turned into a block of winter ice and frozen around her heart. "How could you?"

"How could I what?" His voice was the same as she remembered, but the man in front of her seemed more a stranger than her dearest betrothed.

Of course they weren't really betrothed. They had an understanding between them, but Asher had never approached her pa. Maybe now she knew why.

"We are as good as promised. How could you betray me with that. . .that woman?"

The face which had once been more familiar to her than her own lost its frown. One corner of his mouth turned up in the crooked smile that she remembered so well. "Don't be silly, Rebekah. She's just a girl I met and shared a dance with."

"Just a girl. . ." Rebekah could hear the tremble in her voice. She took a deep breath to steady it. "You were so focused on her that you didn't recognize me. She is obviously more—"

"Oh Rebekah, you're exaggerating the whole thing. It's a simple misunderstanding. I helped her a couple of weeks ago, and she told her pa, who insisted that we dance. Of course I recognized you, but it was such a shock to see you here that it took me a moment to react."

He seemed earnest. Rebekah searched his eyes for some clue, some hint of deception. This was not how she had imagined their reunion at all, but suddenly her heart began to thump wildly. It was a giddy feeling, being so close to him after all this time. And he might have changed, but he was still the same where it counted, wasn't he? He did still love her—she could see it in his face.

Asher reached into his coat pocket and produced a handkerchief that he used to gently dab at her cheeks. "All better now?"

Rebekah nodded. She stood still and let him minister to her. It felt so wonderful, just the way she had known it would. Everything was going to be okay. They were together now, and she would not allow anything to come between them again.

"Asher? Asher, what's wrong? Why did you leave the ball—"

Rebekah sprang away from her beloved as if he had suddenly sprouted porcupine quills. Asher turned to face the woman, shielding Rebekah as she composed herself.

"Alexandra, I didn't mean to worry you. It's just that I saw someone I had not expected to see. Please allow me to introduce someone very special to me. In fact, she is the woman who holds my heart. . .Miss Rebekah Taylor."

Rebekah stepped to one side and looked at the woman who had started the whole thing. Now that she saw her up close, she realized that the woman was even more beautiful than she had first thought. Although Asher's words should have reassured her, she couldn't help wondering what he could see in her if a woman like this was pursuing him.

"Rebekah"—Asher's voice wrapped around her like a blanket—"I want you to meet the daughter of one of our officers, Miss Alexandra Lewis."

"Hello, Miss Taylor." The woman's voice had a curious twist. Wonderful. Even her sultry voice hinted at hidden secrets.

"Miss Lewis." Rebekah nodded her head in acknowledgment of the introduction.

"I don't believe I've ever seen you around here, Miss Taylor."

Asher cleared his throat. "Rebekah, I've never been more shocked than when I realized you were in New Orleans. When did you arrive? How did you get here? Who is chaperoning you?"

Rebekah felt like the two of them were attacking her. Her head was still trying to sort out the facts while her heart had been wrung out like laundry. "I. . .we. . .Aunt Dolly. . .I mean Dolly and Rachel. . .yesterday. We got here yesterday. We came down by boat because General Jackson sent for his wife and son."

She intercepted a glance between Asher and the other woman. What did it mean? She put a hand to her head. "I'm afraid I'm overwrought. Perhaps—"

"Rebekah," another voice interrupted her, "where have you gotten off to, child? Your parents would skin me alive if I didn't keep an eye on you and your young. . ." Dolly's voice trailed off as she took in the three of them.

Rebekah handed Asher's handkerchief back to him and lifted her skirt slightly. "I'm coming, Dolly." She turned to go, but Asher held his arm out. She had to either ignore him or accept his escort. And if she didn't accept his arm, would he offer it to *her*?

Rebekah's hand virtually flew to his arm, and she allowed Asher to lead her into the ballroom, while *she* was left to follow behind.

six

Dolly sat at the window seat, her fingers tracing the dog-eared edges of the magazine in her lap. "It's so difficult to keep up with the latest fashions since *The Lady's Miscellany* stopped publication."

"I know, but perhaps they will resume printing their magazine now that the war is over." Rebekah didn't think her aunt's complaint had anything to do with clothing styles. "How are you feeling?"

Dolly smiled, but it was a weak gesture. "I must be getting too old for all this gadding about."

"I'm glad we turned down the invitation to breakfast. It gives us time to rest." Rebekah folded a blouse and placed it on top of the skirt. The past weeks had been filled with activities. Fancy breakfasts drifting into fancier luncheons. Afternoon soirees on the banks of the Mississippi. Then quick naps to keep up their strength and off again to attend a ceremonial ball or formal dinner party.

It was no wonder her aunt looked so worn out. They both needed to get back to Nashville where life made more sense. The Jackson family had left several days ago, but Aunt Dolly's cough had been so bad that they had decided to remain an extra week in the hopes that the weather would be more salutary during their journey.

"Rest? You're working harder than most maids I've hired."

"I don't mind, Dolly. Not if it means we'll be able to leave soon."

Paper crinkled as Dolly flipped the pages in her magazine.

"I know our accommodations are not the best, but are you so miserable here?"

"Not miserable. . .but I do miss home. And I have to admit I wouldn't care if I never saw another lady's fan again." Rebekah rolled her eyes, pleased when her aunt laughed. In their months together, they had forged a friendship she treasured. Sometimes she had to remind herself that Dolly was her ma's sister—she seemed closer to Rebekah's age than her ma's.

"I know what you mean." Dolly's voice interrupted her musings. "It is amazing, though, how much use we get from them." She fanned her fingers in front of her mouth and fluttered her eyelids as if flirting with an imaginary beau.

Rebekah giggled at her aunt's posturing. "That's precisely my point."

"Are you sure your displeasure is with all the ladies we've met?" Her aunt sent a pointed gaze her direction. "Or is there one particular miss who has gained your ire?"

Rebekah could feel the blush heating her cheeks. Was it so obvious? She could have happily pulled out every dark hair on Miss Alexandra Lewis's head for spending so much time trying to capture Asher's attention. Rebekah had tried and tried to bury her resentment, but it was beyond her ability to do so. "It's just that I hardly ever get to see Asher. And those Lewises seem to be at every party we attend."

"They are very well received," her aunt agreed. "You must know that Captain Landon only has eyes for you, no matter how much that young lady throws herself at him."

Rebekah shook her head. "Asher says he only spends time with her family because her pa is close to the general and has promised to help him attain a promotion."

"I see nothing wrong with that. He is obviously looking out for the future, a future that he wishes to share with you."

"If that is the real reason, then it seems he would also

spend time with us. After all, Rachel is the general's wife. Winning her admiration would probably advance him faster than the efforts of some pretentious local planter."

Dolly tsked her disapproval. "You are not very charitable toward Colonel Lewis. He and his wife are well connected by all accounts. I understand that their families own land up and down the river."

Heat filled her cheeks again. "You are right, but I cannot help thinking that Asher is ashamed of Rachel Jackson. You know how all these people whisper about her and make us all uncomfortable with their barbed words. If Asher were not influenced by people like the Lewises, perhaps he could have led the way to showing all of them Rachel's true worth. And then she might have convinced the general to wait an extra week so we could all travel home together."

Silence fell in the room. When her aunt failed to comment, Rebekah returned to her work. "Are you sure you feel all right?"

Dolly's eyes regained their focus. "Perhaps it is because he does not want to use a woman's influence to further his career."

Rebekah's brows drew together in a frown. "Do you think so?"

Dolly nodded. "I am sure of it. And besides, you need to remember that all of your worries will soon be groundless. Since the general arranged to send us home with a whole host of strong soldiers, including your Asher, Miss Lewis will soon be nothing but an unpleasant memory."

The knot in Rebekah's stomach seemed to diminish at her aunt's assurances. Once they were headed back north, Asher would forget all about Alexandra Lewis and her connections. Then things would get back to normal. Finally she and Asher could continue planning their future together.

A knock drew the ladies' attention.

Dolly got up and went to the door. "Yes."

The words of their visitor were inaudible, but Rebekah heard her aunt's response. "I see. Tell our guest we'll be down in a few moments."

When her aunt shut the door and turned around, Rebekah sighed. She didn't know if she could continue being polite to the local gentry. They were too different from the folks at home. "I can finish the packing while you go downstairs."

"Nonsense. You'll want to see this visitor." Dolly seemed more animated, her eyes twinkling as if she knew a wondrous secret.

Rebekah's heart leaped upward. "Asher?"

Her aunt nodded, and Rebekah instantly reached to check that her hair was not mussed. She smoothed her calico skirt, wishing she'd worn something prettier and not quite so practical this morning.

"You look fine, dear." Dolly's voice calmed her nerves.

Rebekah stopped fussing with her appearance as an idea occurred to her. "Do you think it would be okay to give him his gift now?"

Dolly nodded. "I think this is the perfect time to do so!"

Rebekah smiled, retrieved the package, and followed Dolly to the parlor downstairs. Asher had finally come to see her! She pushed back her discontent; she was determined to enjoy his visit.

The broad window that took up one wall of the parlor outlined her beloved's straight shoulders. He turned and smiled as she entered the room, and Rebekah's heart fluttered. He was so handsome. She sent God a quick prayer of thanks that Asher loved her. And a request that He would smooth the pathway for their marriage. She couldn't wait until they were husband and wife—then they could talk every day.

Dolly greeted Asher before taking a seat in one corner of the room and turning her attention to the magazine she'd brought from their suite.

Asher took Rebekah's hand and enveloped it gently. "How have you been, sweetheart?"

Rebekah smiled at his endearment. "Fine."

Dolly cleared her throat, causing Rebekah to pull her hand out of Asher's warm grasp. "I have something for you." She held out the gift.

Asher took it from her and unwrapped the cloth with a quick motion. "Look! What a fine handkerchief. And you stitched my initials on it, too. What a talented seamstress you are."

"I hope you like it."

"How could I not, when you made it especially for me." He smiled, and her heart did a little jump. "Thank you so much, Rebekah."

"You are most welcome." She sat gingerly on the edge of the striped sofa that was stationed at the far end of the room from Dolly. The sun outside was brighter, and she felt like laughing out loud. Her whole world seemed to have changed in a matter of moments as she had gone from worrying about Asher's preoccupation to basking in his admiration. Asher's love and approval were the only things that mattered.

"I missed seeing you at the Dupree breakfast." Asher settled himself beside her on the sofa, but he left a respectable distance between them.

"Dolly and I decided to stay here and begin our packing." Rebekah realized she was twisting her hands together and consciously relaxed them in her lap. A lady was not supposed to broadcast her feelings. Another of those silly society rules.

Asher cleared his throat, and she turned her gaze up to his face. "I'm certain you ladies are exhausted with all the social occasions. And you will need all of your strength for the journey home. In fact, that's one of the reasons I was looking for you this morning. I have news to share."

Her heart became an icicle. "From home?"

Asher shook his head. "No, but I'm sure everyone is fine back home. This has more to do with our upcoming trip. It seems you will have a traveling companion. Someone of your own age."

Rebekah tried to hide the disappointment that rose in her as she realized this might hinder her time with Asher.

"The Lewises and their daughter." Asher paused and glanced down at her. "Do you remember Alexandra Lewis?"

Surely he couldn't mean...

"She's a sweet thing. I'm sure you will be the best of friends."

His words brought a gasp of dismay that she covered with a cough. She knew he was watching her, so she pinned what she hoped was a convincing smile on her lips. No need to tell him how she felt about Alexandra. He might even try to defend her rival, and Rebekah could not abide that. What could she say? "How...nice. I'm sure we will...find something...in common."

Asher patted her hand. "You are the sweetest girl in the world."

She didn't feel very sweet. She felt as deceitful as Delilah. A burning sensation made her blink her eyes rapidly. She would *not* deceive the man she loved. In that instant, Rebekah decided to do everything she could to deserve Asher's praise. She would find something to like about Alexandra Lewis—no matter what it cost her.

seven

The next morning, Rebekah's vow was immediately put to the test when she found out they would be sharing their wagon with Alexandra and her mother. Was God trying to test her? She had never dreamed that the Lewis family would not have their own wagon. Instead of having to put up with Alexandra during meals, she would be subjected to her every day, all day long, for the entire trip.

She looked at the wagon, trying to decide whether there was any chance for privacy. It was nearly twenty feet long from the tip of the tongue to the gated back, but the area where the four women would travel facing each other for the next month was the bed of the wagon—a space of some five by eight feet. It was topped with bent poles that would be covered with heavy, oiled canvas for most of the trip. The inside was fitted with two long benches that had been covered with padding for their comfort. Underneath the benches was room to store a few bags containing basic necessities, but most of their clothing would follow in the provisions wagon.

Rebekah glanced longingly toward the men on horseback. Why did she have to be relegated to the wagon like a sack of meal? She could ride as well as Asher and would have been glad to show her ability if not for the ridiculous strictures placed on women by society's conventions.

Alexandra and her mother had already made themselves comfortable on one side of the wagon. Rebekah forced the corners of her mouth up and waited as Aunt Dolly was helped into the wagon.

"Bonju," Mrs. Lewis greeted them with the accent so prevalent in New Orleans. She was an older version of her daughter—a slight woman with dark hair and eyes and an air of sophistication that Rebekah wished she could emulate. "I am so happy to see you both again. I think we met at one of the victory celebrations. We are honored to travel north with you to your home."

Aunt Dolly stowed her leather satchel and held her hand out to Mrs. Lewis. "It is a pleasure to see you again, also. We look forward to becoming the best of friends before we arrive in Nashville."

Best of friends? Rebekah had serious doubts whether she would be able to maintain the appearance of civility.

But Aunt Dolly did not seem to share her misgivings. As the wagon headed north, she chatted with Mrs. Lewis about everything from the defeat of the British to the latest reports of bandit gangs on the northern route to Nashville.

Rebekah turned slightly to watch as the riverfront gave way to forest, wishing they were at the end of their journey rather than the beginning.

"Miss Taylor. . ." Alexandra's whisper drew her attention away from the scenery.

"Yes, Miss Lewis?"

"I hope you don't mind our company on your trip to Nashville. Surely you are not envious because Asher has been visiting my home so much."

What could she say? She did not want to be rude, but she could not lie either. It was obvious to her that Alexandra was interested in having more than a casual friendship with Asher. A shrug was all she could manage.

"That Asher. . ." Mrs. Lewis's comment was a welcome interruption. "The colonel believes he will make an excellent officer."

"Yes, he has been very loyal to his country, staying past his original obligation." Aunt Dolly leaned forward and smiled toward her. "Our Rebekah has proved herself to be the perfect mate for Asher by the way she has patiently awaited his return and traveled into the wilderness to see him when he couldn't come home."

The topic of their conversation must have heard his name. He pulled his horse even with the wagon. "Are you ladies comfortable?"

Aunt Dolly answered for them. "We are quite content. Thank you for arranging this large wagon we can share."

Asher's shoulders straightened. "We have a cover to protect you from the weather, too."

Alexandra opened her fan. "You've thought of everything, Captain Landon."

"Thank you, Miss Lewis, but your father deserves part of the credit, too."

"Yes." Mrs. Lewis nodded. "The colonel is a good husband. He is always thinking of our comfort."

Asher saluted the ladies before riding to the front of their cavalcade to scout the pathway ahead.

As Mrs. Lewis continued to sing the praises of the colonel, Rebekah played with the fringe of her bonnet. Until they put the cover up, it would protect her skin from the sunshine. She peered upward through the thick canopy of pine trees. Of course, if the forest remained this dense, she would have little need for either. But what would shield her from watching Alexandra Lewis flirt with Asher?

❧

"I would really like to reach the Natchez Road before day's end. Our journey from New Orleans has been uneventful so far, but I'm not sure if it's a good idea to take a detour. How many days would it cost us?" Asher watched Colonel Lewis sharpen his razor on a strip of leather.

The colonel frowned as he began to shave in the reflection

of a mirror he had propped on the low branch of a dogwood tree. "We could be there by midday, and we'd resume our journey in a day or two, as soon as everyone is rested. Our ladies need a respite from these primitive conditions."

Asher looked around at their campsite, ringed by leafless, moss-hung oak trees. Alexandra and the older ladies, all of whom were accustomed to the modern conveniences of city life, could not be comfortable sleeping out in the open with only the underside of a wagon for shelter. His Rebekah, of course, thrived in any conditions, but she would probably enjoy a little extra pampering as well.

He brushed the sleeve of his uniform with a fond smile. Rebekah had done a good job mending the tear in it. "If you think the ladies would like it, I suppose we could take a side trip."

"Excellent." Colonel Lewis trimmed his mustache. "I know you're anxious to be home, but I think we will all enjoy staying with the Tanner family. My wife has received several letters from her widowed mother, but she'll be elated to see her again."

Asher realized he actually looked forward to the respite as well. Just as he'd enjoyed many times in New Orleans, he delighted in seeing his Rebekah ensconced in the society in which he dreamed they would one day belong.

eight

"You're a handsome young man, and as mannerly as you are good looking. I imagine half the girls in the territory are trying to turn your head." Mrs. Althea Tanner's voice was strident and forceful, her words drawing a snicker from the assorted relatives who were seating themselves at the formal dining table.

Asher could feel his ears heating up from her comments as he helped Alexandra's grandmother to the table. She leaned her hickory cane against the arm of her chair and grabbed his sleeve. Asher was anxious to get to Rebekah, but he had no choice except to lean over the older lady. Her skin was so thin it was almost translucent, but he did not make the mistake of thinking her senile. Although her brown eyes had faded to the color of buckskins, they were as sharp as a hunter's.

"Don't be embarrassed. When you get as old as I am, you learn to speak your mind and accept whatever compliments come your way."

"Yes, ma'am."

Mrs. Tanner pointed to the seat on her right. "Sit here next to me." She waved away the son who most likely considered the seat his and looked at her granddaughter, who was hovering in the background. "You may sit on his other side, Alexandra."

Asher threw an apologetic glance toward Rebekah. Dismay was plain on her face, but what could he do? They should be sitting together farther down the table. The seats next to Grandma Tanner should be occupied by Alexandra and her parents, followed by the host of Alexandra's relatives who lived on the extensive plantation. But in the hours since their arrival at Tanner Plantation, he had quickly learned that Mrs. Tanner ruled her family with all the authority of a royal queen. Etiquette did not matter—only the wishes of the matriarch. He pulled out a chair for Alexandra on his right and took the seat between her and her grandmother.

Colonel Lewis offered a gruff blessing, and the unobtrusive slaves began to serve the food.

The first course was a thick, white soup. Asher picked up his spoon and tried it, his smile deepening at the wonderful flavor of fresh corn. "Delicious."

"Thank you." Mrs. Tanner inclined her head, reminding him again of royalty. "We grow all the ingredients right here on our land, from the spices to the corn in that chowder. In fact, I am proud to say that we either grow, raise, or catch nearly everything we eat. There's little we need to barter for. Not like those who live in the big cities and rely on others to supply their needs. But then, we are not quite so hard-pressed for our survival as those of you living on the frontier."

Asher nodded his agreement and looked down the table toward Rebekah. He was relieved to see she had been seated next to her aunt. He would have liked the opportunity to converse with her, tell her how proud he was of her efforts during their journey. Even though they had both been very busy on the trip—he with securing their safety, she with making the travelers as comfortable as possible—he felt like they had been working in tandem. It was like practice for being married.

Once they were man and wife, they would have different responsibilities, but it would take both of them to become successful. He had such hopes that he could make a contribution to the development of the United States. These were confusing days, and he knew it would take men with boldness and clear vision to make the important decisions that would secure America's future. He wanted to be one of those men. And with a woman like Rebekah by his side, he could succeed.

Alexandra's voice brought him out of his reverie. "That's a terrible frown you have on your face, Captain Landon."

"I'm sorry. I was thinking of home."

Alexandra put her spoon down beside her bowl. "Tell me about Nashville."

"It is certainly not an important metropolitan center like New Orleans, but the land there is breathtakingly beautiful. I'd venture to say it is the most beautiful part of the world with its majestic trees and sparkling streams. The Cumberland River that flows around Nashville is narrower than the Mississippi, with clear, swift water and fish that are longer than my arm."

"You make it sound wonderful."

Nostalgia tugged at Asher's heart. The past year and a half had been eventful—and he would never trade the experience those months had brought him—but he was glad to finally be going home. "My favorite time of the day is early evening when the sun drops down on the far side of the hills. The stars begin to appear one by one until the whole sky looks as bright as that chandelier. Even the trees seem to whisper that God is greater than man can conceive as the wind blows across their branches in the evening. When I look at the forests and realize that God put them there years before I was born and that they will be there long after I am gone, it puts my problems into perspective."

"You are quite poetic, Captain."

Asher laughed, a little embarrassed that he had allowed them to see his love for home. "It's been a long time since I've been there, Miss Lewis."

❧

Rebekah lost count of the courses that were served at the Tanner dinner table. It seemed there was more food than would be needed to supply General Jackson's whole army for a week—including the Baratarian pirates. She picked at the meat on her plate and wondered if the interminable dinner would ever end.

Things could not be worse. Asher was sitting at the head of the table, laughing with their hostess and *that woman*. How dare he enjoy himself when she was trapped next to some portentous old man who did nothing more than burp and belch his way through dinner.

With a sigh, she turned her attention to Aunt Dolly. "How are you feeling?"

"Much better." Dolly yawned behind the cover of her hand. "But I am still quite ready for a return to that comfortable bed."

Rebekah was relieved that her aunt was looking much less wilted. At least she could be thankful for that. The last thing she wanted was for her aunt to suffer a relapse. "I wonder if we should stay here a day or two before we resume our journey."

Dolly rolled her eyes. "I'm ready to get home. It's taken so much longer than I'd thought. And I'm not an invalid, you know. Sometimes you are too solicitous of my health. I'll be ready to go as soon as your Asher says it is time."

Rebekah would have challenged her aunt's characterization of Captain Asher Landon, but the scraping of chairs against the dining room's pine floor alerted them that dinner was officially over. She could not resist a glance toward the head of the table to see if Asher would come to escort them to the parlor, but he seemed to have all of his attention taken by a certain dark-haired temptress.

Rebekah pasted a smile on her face and laughed as if Aunt Dolly had said something terribly funny. Aunt Dolly and the old codger were both looking at her oddly, but she shook her head and proceeded to the parlor.

There was a fireplace in the room, and Rebekah was

thankful there was no fire lit. Sometimes people as old as Mrs. Tanner liked to keep fires burning no matter how warm the weather. In front of the fireplace stood a tall-backed chair that resembled a throne. Instinctively, she looked toward Asher, catching his eye. It was as if they could communicate without words.

He tipped his head slightly toward the chair, and she nodded. They both smiled. It felt wonderful. Maybe he had not changed so much after all. Maybe there was hope for her dreams.

More relatives kept coming into the room. The Tanner household was certainly extensive, which explained why they lived in such an enormous house. She was sure she would get lost and never be found again if she wandered away from the parlor on her own. The house was even larger than the hotel in New Orleans and must be three or four times the size of Aunt Dolly's home.

She thought back to the day when her pa had first taken her to Nashville to care for her aunt. She'd never imagined she would spend the night in a home that made that house seem small in comparison. It was odd how things changed one's perspective.

Mrs. Tanner took her seat and waved a hand toward her granddaughter. "Alexandra, why don't you play for us?"

"I would be happy to, *Grand-mère*. But I will need some help with the pages."

Rebekah watched as Alexandra turned toward Asher. Surely he would not. . . . But he did. He walked over and helped Alexandra at the piano as she fussed with everything—her skirts, the music, the stool. Finally, it seemed she was ready to perform.

Rebekah clenched her teeth. Things had certainly gone from bad to worse. She tapped one foot and wished the evening would end so she could go to bed. Then it would be morning and they could leave.

Mrs. Tanner's strident voice cut across the polite applause after Alexandra finished her piece. "Why don't you play something for us, Miss Taylor?"

Rebekah's attention jerked back to the older lady. "Oh, no." She could not believe the suggestion. She looked around to see that she was the center of attention. Her heart pounded so hard she thought she might pass out. There was no way she could push any more words past her frozen throat.

"Perhaps Miss Taylor is shy." Alexandra's sultry voice quieted the hubbub of speculation from her relatives. "But we are all friends here." She stood up and took a vacant seat on the sofa next to her grandmother. "Perhaps she needs some of you to encourage her to perform for us."

Aunt Dolly raised her hand to get their attention. "Rebekah is not shy." Her voice remained calm and assured. "She does not play the piano."

Someone gasped. Rebekah heard one of the women talking. "How can any young lady's parents so neglect her education?"

Rebekah desperately wished she were somewhere—anywhere—else. She wished she'd never heard of Tanner Plantation, much less met any of Alexandra's relatives. This is what came of trying to pass herself off as a society miss when she did not possess the right accomplishments. She shook her head, wishing the nightmare would end. She wanted to crawl under her chair and never come out again. Perhaps she should lose herself in the mansion.

Aunt Dolly came to her rescue again. "I know it's different here, but in Nashville, we don't spend as much time worrying about teaching our young ladies how to sing or play the piano. We think it's more important that they know how to survive and how to help others in need. Rebekah Taylor has nursed me back to health with her loving care and medicinal potions. Furthermore, she has spent the last year keeping an entire household running smoothly. And if you could taste one of the apple pies she bakes, you would understand the meaning of real talent."

Gasps and titters followed Aunt Dolly's words, and the elder Mrs. Tanner harrumphed her obvious disapproval of such plebeian accomplishments.

"Come along, dear." Dolly's hand felt warm around her fingers. "I think I need a bit of fresh air."

As they left the parlor, Rebekah thought she heard Mrs. Tanner saying something about manners and hospitality, but she was too distraught to make sense of it. She followed her aunt onto the wide porch.

"Breathe, Rebekah," Dolly said.

Rebekah nodded and concentrated on filling her lungs. After a few moments, her heartbeat returned to a more normal rhythm. "Thank you, Dolly."

"Silly girl, you can't let people like that affect you so."

The words were said with so much love that Rebekah felt some of her shame easing. She was not happy she'd had to rely on her aunt for defense, but at least Aunt Dolly had come to her rescue. Asher, on the other hand, had remained silent. Didn't he love her enough to protect her reputation?

As if her thoughts had summoned him, Asher stepped onto the porch. "Are you okay, Rebekah?"

"I believe I hear someone calling me." Dolly squeezed her hand and placed it on the rail. "I'll be right inside if either of you needs me."

Silence filled the night as Rebekah concentrated again on her breathing. She gripped the railing so tightly that she wondered if it would break under the pressure. "I want to go home."

He was standing right behind her, so close she could smell his pomade. She wanted to turn and bury herself in his arms, but she could not. Not until they talked about the matter of his attraction to Alexandra.

"I know you do, sweetheart. And I want to get you home. Get back to where we were before this war started. You have only been away from Nashville for a few months. It has been nearly two years for me."

His words sparked another point of contention. "Yet you passed up the chance to come home earlier."

"It wasn't like that, Rebekah. General Jackson gave me a special assignment. I was proud to serve him and our country. But because of that assignment, I had no real choice."

His words melted away one of the resentments she had held against Asher. She turned and looked up at him. "What kind of assignment?"

He put a finger on her nose. "The secret kind, my curious girl."

Rebekah pushed away his hand. She supposed she would have to accept his answer. She knew there were things men could not talk about in regard to their military service. The same had been true of her pa. Her ma had told her years ago that there were some things it was better to leave alone.

But Alexandra Lewis was another matter entirely.

"Do you still love me?" She was glad that her eyes had adjusted to the darkness around them. She could see every expression on his face, the face she loved more than any other.

"What?"

The first thing she saw was confusion, followed swiftly by disbelief and then humor. What she did not see was shame or deceit. So maybe he was still in love with her. . .and not Alexandra. But that still did not appease her. "You know she is trying to entrap you."

"Who? Alexandra?" He laughed. "She's like a little sister. Always getting into trouble and needing someone to guide her. She does not feel anything toward me except the love a sister feels toward a big brother."

Rebekah pointed a finger at his chest. "That's where you're wrong. You mark my words, Asher Landon. Alexandra Lewis does not think of you as a brother. She thinks of you as a suitor. And if you're not careful, she'll get you into a compromising position and rely on your chivalry to trap you."

"I cannot believe you, Rebekah. I thought you knew me better than that. You are the only girl who interests me at all. Ten Alexandras could not hold a candle to you. You're the only girl I've ever asked to marry me."

"And yet we are not married."

"As soon as we get back to Nashville, that will change. I'll go to your parents the very first day and procure their blessing. Then as soon as I can buy or build us a home, you will become Mrs. Asher Landon."

Rebekah longed to embrace his words and cling to their promise, but even though she forced a smile to her face, her heart hid a cloud of concern for the future.

nine

Rain drenched the canvas sides of their wagon, bringing a steady, cold breeze that chilled the travelers and made Rebekah wish for an early summer. Mrs. Lewis and Alexandra were sleeping on the bench opposite where she cuddled close to Aunt Dolly.

Rebekah stretched her right hand to push back the heavy cloth covering the wagon's back gate and peered out at the tall pines standing like silent pickets on both sides of the muddy track. The separate wagon holding their clothes and provisions trundled into view around a bend.

A flash in the underbrush drew her attention. Out of the corner of her eye, she saw another swift movement. She jerked her head around but spotted nothing. Was someone hiding behind one of the large tree trunks, or was she imagining things? "Wake up, Dolly."

"What, dear?" Aunt Dolly's voice was slow and thick. She stretched her arms forward and yawned.

"I'm sorry to disturb you, but I thought I saw something in the woods."

Neither of the Lewis ladies roused, but the soldier who was driving the wagon turned around and placed a silencing finger over his lips.

Rebekah's heart began to thump heavily. Only a few days of travel separated them from Nashville, and the trip thus far had been uneventful. The dreary weather had been their greatest trial. It had rained on them nearly every day since leaving Tanner Plantation, turning the road into a muddy path and placing an extra burden on the men and horses.

Rebekah held her breath and prayed for safety. A bird whistled in the distance, answered by another that sounded closer to their wagon. A bush alongside the road trembled as though caught in a strong wind. She looked upward, but the branches of the tall pines were still.

She was nearly thrown to the floor when their horses were brought to an unexpected halt. Both Alexandra and Mrs. Lewis woke abruptly, their voices sharp inside the wagon.

A small scream escaped Aunt Dolly, but Rebekah refused to give way to the panic building inside her. Instead she looked around for some type of weapon to use. Her sewing basket and Aunt Dolly's jewelry box were the only items she saw.

Mrs. Lewis put one hand over her heart and grasped Alexandra's arm with the other. "What's happening? Is it bandits?"

"Could be." Their driver reached back for the musket leaning against the seat and laid it across his knees. "All I know for sure is someone wants us to stop."

Rebekah looked from one lady to the other, her mind grappling with the implications. Was the situation that desperate? She hoped not. Yet who had not heard of travelers meeting their demise along the road to Nashville?

The sharp report of gunfire punctuated her thoughts. The horses whinnied and fought to get away from the noise, making the wagon rock back and forth violently as the driver tried to calm them. Something thudded against the side of the canvas wall. Another *thud*. Rebekah realized it was the sound of arrows striking the sides of the wagon. Indians!

Aunt Dolly slid to the floor and gestured for the rest of the women to join her. "Lord, protect us." Her voice was calm, as if she were sitting in a church pew at home rather than on a dusty wooden floor in the middle of a forest full of dangerous Indians.

Were they about to be scalped? Burned to death? Rebekah

squeezed her eyes shut and tried to pray along with Aunt Dolly and the others, but her mind was in a dither. The noise was horrendous—she could hear screaming from the servants in the other wagon, wild cries from the Indians, and the men shouting back and forth to each other. *Lord, save us.*

Rebekah opened her eyes. She had to see what was going on outside. She thought about the empty cart she and her pa had seen when he first took her to stay with Aunt Dolly. Would some other traveler come across their empty wagon in a few days and wonder what had happened to them? She could not hear any more thuds against the sides, but that was because the rushing noise of her pulse was blocking out all other sounds.

She watched as Aunt Dolly lifted her head slightly to gaze over the wooden back of the driver's seat.

"What's happening?" Rebekah wished her words sounded as calm as Aunt Dolly's had. She took a deep, calming breath and released it slowly. The noise outside had definitely abated.

"They're talking to the Indians. Something about a storm. I can see Asher shaking his head, but I can't hear what he's saying."

A heartfelt praise lifted the worst of the fear from Rebekah's mind. At least he'd not been harmed. And she had no doubt he could calm the situation. She rubbed her aunt's cold hand. "Everything's going to be all right."

Their horses began to quiet as if they also sensed that the greatest danger had passed.

The minutes seemed to stretch out as the four women waited for the confrontation to end. Aunt Dolly pushed herself up onto the seat. "I'm going to see exactly what's going on. The rest of you stay here."

"Do you think that's wise?" Mrs. Lewis's question echoed Rebekah's thoughts.

"It may not be wise, but I cannot cower in here any longer."

Aunt Dolly clambered onto the driver's seat before climbing down and disappearing from Rebekah's view.

Rebekah and Alexandra helped Mrs. Lewis back up onto the seat now that the most immediate danger had passed. The men's voices moved around to the back of the wagon, and Rebekah scooted down the bench to the gate. She separated the heavy, wet material protecting them to watch the confrontation.

Asher had dismounted and was standing next to his horse, his rifle held loosely in one hand. His stance seemed odd, but maybe it was only her imagination.

A slight sound behind the wagon to her right made her wonder if they were completely surrounded by Indians. Rebekah leaned against the wooden gate, trying to understand what was being said.

When an unseen hand pulled the bolt free on the gate, it fell open and she fell with it, tumbling out and landing on the muddy road with a jaw-cracking *thump*. Rebekah was so surprised she didn't even cry out. Someone grabbed her arm and jerked her back onto her feet. She twisted her head and looked into the darkest brown eyes she'd ever seen—eyes that mirrored her own fear.

He was an Indian brave, but he couldn't have been more than twelve years old. Her shocked gaze took in his buckskin attire and straight black hair. Somehow, when she thought of the danger of Indians, they were full-grown adults, not boys who were young enough to be in short pants.

Rebekah's fear melted away. This was not some faceless danger. This was a person, someone who had hopes and dreams and fears, just like she did. Her thoughts were cut off, however, when he jerked his head to indicate that she should join the others who were still having a somewhat heated debate.

". . .no food." Asher's words were clipped, and his voice

sounded harsh to Rebekah. He turned and saw the Indian brave guiding her forward. "Don't you put your filthy hands on her."

"It's okay, Asher. He's not hurting—"

Aunt Dolly's voice cut off her protest. "I thought you were going to stay inside."

"I thought so, too." Rebekah glanced down at her muddy dress. "But I sort of fell out."

Asher strode to her and pulled her from the Indian's grasp. "Are you hurt?"

"Only my dignity."

He smiled his crooked half smile, and the others faded to nothingness. She forgot the cold and the danger. Asher was the only thing that mattered. But then he turned his attention back to the discussion at hand, and reality returned in the form of cold raindrops sliding down her back.

She listened to the debate between the men, her sympathy roused as the Indians' desperation became apparent. It had been a difficult winter made harder by the influx of white settlers who competed for the wild game in the area. At first, this tribe had tried to trade with the newcomers, but they had been met with distrust and hatred. Unable to overcome the settlers' fears, they had turned to other means to provide for their families.

"Maybe the hatred was earned." Colonel Lewis pointed at the Indian. "Maybe you took a few scalps along the way."

The man who seemed to be the spokesperson for the band of Indians shook his head. "We want peace with you." He was tall and straight, with shoulders as wide as her pa's and with the bearing she associated with military men such as Asher and General Jackson.

Aunt Dolly let out an unladylike snort. "I might find that easier to believe if you had not attacked us today."

"Do you see dead white men?" The Indian raised his chin.

"If we really attack, all the men die, and we take you back to our village."

Rebekah could not help the shudder that passed through her. The Indian's words painted an awful picture in her mind—Asher lying on the ground with an arrow piercing his heart, his lifeblood staining the ground as she was dragged away to face unimaginable hardship. She grasped Asher's hand.

"If you want peace, return to your village." Asher squeezed her hand before releasing it. "Don't you see that stopping people and stealing from them will bring nothing but more death and hatred?"

"And what do we tell our starving women and children? Do we tell them to suffer so the white man will be our friend?"

Rebekah could hear the pain in his voice. There must be something they could do to help his people. "Don't we have some extra provisions we can give them?"

"Have you lost your mind, girl?" Colonel Lewis frowned at her. "Do you want to take the chance of starving yourself by giving away our food?"

"Rebekah is right, Colonel." Aunt Dolly's voice was as calm as it had been in the wagon. "We have more than enough to last for the final week of our journey. There is a full wagon of canned vegetables and flour sacks traveling with us. I think we can share our bounty. It is our Christian duty to do so."

"Christian duty? Where does the Good Book say we should feed the heathens who attack our farms and kill innocent women and children?"

"I believe it's in the book of Matthew. Jesus said, 'But I say unto you, Love your enemies, bless them that curse you, do good to them that hate you, and pray for them which despitefully use you, and persecute you.'"

The colonel's face turned as red as an autumn sunset. "The next thing you'll say is that we should give them all of our food and let God provide manna like He did for the

Hebrews in the wilderness. This is men's business. You should both get back to the wagon."

Rebekah wished she could remain as calm as Aunt Dolly, who managed to keep a smile on her face as she answered the colonel. "I am not accustomed to bowing to the 'wisdom' of belligerence and intimidation."

Asher cleared his throat and stepped in front of Colonel Lewis. The Indians raised their bows in response, but he ignored them. "Why don't we see if we can share our provisions? It's obvious we are outnumbered, and it would be wiser to share rather than provoke these men into taking everything." His voice dropped so low that Rebekah could barely make out the quiet words he directed to the colonel. "There will be a better time than today to show our strength."

A tense moment passed while the colonel and Asher stared at each other. Then the colonel nodded. "Do what you must." He turned on his heel and pushed his way past the braves, who still held their weapons ready.

The Indian who had spoken to them turned back to the rest of the raiding party and addressed his men in staccato words. They lowered their weapons and stepped back, but Rebekah had the feeling they were still poised to attack if anything went wrong.

Asher and the Indian leader went back to the wagon that held their provisions.

Aunt Dolly turned to Rebekah. "You're shivering, Rebekah. And no wonder. Standing out here in the rain is beyond foolish."

"You must be cold, too."

Aunt Dolly nodded. "I believe your Asher has everything under control. Let's get back into the wagon where the wind will not cut us in two. We'll be none the worse for helping the Indians and on our way again soon."

Once they were inside, Aunt Dolly told the other ladies about the encounter.

Half-listening to her aunt's story, Rebekah's mind wandered to the young Indian lad. What would happen to that boy who had pulled her from the wagon? Would he grow into a hard man filled with hatred for the white man? Was there any chance to forge a bond between his people and her people? Surely there was enough room in this great country for both to coexist.

She thought about the argument she had sparked between Colonel Lewis and Aunt Dolly. He apparently had little understanding of Jesus and His love for others. Then another thought struck her. What about the Indians? Were they saved? Her personal considerations were swept away in a flood of concern. They needed the chance to know Christ as their personal Savior. If caring Christians didn't share the gospel with them, who would? And if they didn't have Christ in their hearts. . .

Rebekah shuddered. Distrust and fear were rampant these days, but with patience and love she prayed it would be possible to bring the two worlds together.

❧

Asher shaded his eyes from the rays of the late-afternoon sun. They would have to set up camp immediately. He wished he could count on Colonel Lewis to help, but the man seemed to have little understanding of the amount of work to be done. Instead of gathering wood or rubbing down the horses, he would spend his time talking to the womenfolk and leave all the chores to Asher and the soldiers driving the wagons.

The ferry bumped against the bank, and he led his horse off of its bobbing surface. Then he dismounted and tied his reins to a convenient branch. Striding back to the ferry, he grabbed the leads of the horses pulling the first wagon to calm them as they negotiated the transition between rushing river and dry ground. By the time both wagons were safe on dry ground, the sun was hanging low in the sky.

The bearded ferryman pulled against the rope that guided him back and forth across the river. "Keep a sharp eye out for Injuns," he shouted across the sound of the rushing water. "I been seein' a lot of them thievin' braves up and down the river last week or so."

Asher waved at the man. It was too bad he couldn't have stated his warning privately instead of shouting it out so all the women would hear. There was no need to cause them undue alarm. They were under his care, and the Good Lord had given him the ability to watch out over them.

A quick survey of the area led him to a pretty meadow about two hundred feet from the bank of the river. He went back to collect the rest of the party and start getting everyone settled in for the night. He had almost finished checking the horses for thorns and stones that might delay their travel when Rebekah walked up.

"Would you like some hot coffee? I brewed it strong the way you like it."

He blew on his frozen hands and reached for the tin cup. "Perfect." He hoped she understood that he wasn't only referring to the beverage she'd brought.

Rebekah's head dipped. He would have liked to continue looking into her eyes. There was so much he wanted to tell her. How thoughts of her had sustained him during their many months of separation. How wonderful it was to be near her now and see her every day.

He also wanted to tell her that he looked forward to building a big home for her right in the center of Nashville. He had big plans that would almost certainly make her the wealthiest woman in Nashville. Once they were married, he would make certain she never had to work hard again.

She could spend all of her time in the company of the most prominent citizens of Nashville.

"I guess I should get back to the fire." She peeked up at him for a brief instant before looking away. "Aunt Dolly will need help preparing supper."

Was she teasing him? Asher gulped down the rest of his coffee and reached for her hand. It felt cold, and he wrapped his fingers around hers to impart some of his warmth to her. "I have a better idea. Why don't we collect the canteens and walk down to the river together?"

"I. . .I don't know if we should."

"Please, Rebekah. We'll be back in Nashville in a few days. . . ."

His heart sped up when she smiled and nodded. "But you have to promise to be a gentleman."

He put a hand over his heart and staggered back a few steps. "You wound me."

They kept up a lighthearted conversation as he led her down the path to the river. In the fading light, the water began to take on a silver sheen. It was wild and beautiful, a fine example of God's handiwork. They filled the canteens and stood quietly enjoying the sounds of nature.

Asher's breath condensed in the cool air. "I've missed home."

Her small hand touched his arm. "I prayed for you every day. I was so afraid you would be killed or maimed. And then after a year when you didn't come home, I thought maybe you'd found a reason to stay away. . . ."

His Rebekah was almost too beautiful for words. He reached out a hand to push back a tendril of her moon-kissed hair. Her eyes closed as if she, too, was overcome by the moment. Her lips parted slightly. She was so close he could feel her breath on his cheek. If he leaned forward just a few more inches, their lips would meet. But he would not ruin this special moment they shared. He backed away.

"Is something wrong?" Her voice, so warm a moment ago, sounded lost.

"No." He turned toward the forest in an attempt to control his turbulent emotions. "You should go back to the others."

"Asher, what is it? Did I say something wrong?" Her voice caught. "Or did you really find a reason to stay away?"

A scream interrupted his thoughts before he could form the right words. He turned and ran into the line of trees while reaching for his pistol. "Who's there?"

"It's me. Alexandra!" Her voice ended on a wail.

"Where are you?" He ran forward until he could make out her shape in the gathering dusk.

"There's something out there." She pointed to a willow tree that was indeed shaking in a most odd fashion.

Asher crept forward, his pistol cocked and ready, his mind filled with images of Indian braves and wild animals. He was a few yards away when the tree tilted toward him. He jumped back, nearly landing on top of Alexandra.

In the clearing where the tree had stood was a large, furry, brown shape standing on its hind legs. As soon as he saw the animal's flat black tail, Asher laughed. "It's only a beaver trying to build a new home."

Alexandra's throaty laughter joined his, and Asher found himself overcome with mirth. He doubled over with large, loud guffaws. It must have been relief that made her laugh with him, but whatever the reason, her giggles were contagious. His chest shook, and his stomach clenched, but he could not control the laughter. He pointed at the confused-looking beaver, which seemed unable to decide whether or not to claim his willow tree, and chortled again.

That's when Rebekah found them laughing together like a couple of demented geese. She shot him a look of pain and pushed past them.

The laughter dried up as suddenly as it had come. He had not meant to hurt Rebekah. He took a step toward her retreating figure, but Alexandra put a hand on his arm.

"Thank you for coming again to my rescue."

Asher nodded and turned away from Alexandra to watch Rebekah until he was sure she was safely back in the camp. He knew he ought to catch up to her and explain things—from why he had turned away from her to why he was laughing with Alexandra. But he had no idea how to put his feelings into words. He reholstered his pistol and returned with Alexandra to the river for the canteens.

As they climbed the pathway through the darkening woods, Asher's vague guilt hardened into a sense of injustice. Did Rebekah expect him to ignore a cry for help? Of course not, but instead of rushing back like an impetuous, spoiled child, she should have stayed with him and Alexandra. They could have explained their laughter, and then all three of them could have traveled together rather than returning to camp separately.

The thought of them traveling separately in life flitted through his mind, but he pushed it away, assuring himself Rebekah wanted the same things he did. *Didn't she?*

ten

Rebekah shifted on the hard wooden bench as the new pastor looked out over the congregation. When Brother Lawrence had died last fall, Aunt Dolly's church, as Rebekah distinguished it in her mind from her home church, had been led by a series of elders. All of them were good men, but the church needed its own shepherd. In response to the church members' prayers, Roman Miller had arrived in Nashville at the beginning of the year, and he and his wife, Una, set to work immediately to serve God's purpose.

Pastor Miller called for a prayer, and Rebekah reined in her attention, focusing on the blessings he asked for the congregation. She added her own prayer for a happy future with Asher. He had not attended service this morning, and she was worried he was ill.

When the prayer was over, the pastor issued an invitation to all new believers to come forward, and the congregation sang the closing hymn. As the last notes died away, Rebekah and Aunt Dolly gathered their cloaks and rose to leave.

Alexandra Lewis and her mother waved to them from across the sanctuary, and Rebekah forced a smile to her lips as she nodded. The dashing young woman seemed the embodiment of every problem in her life. She dropped a glove and slowly picked it up, hoping to avoid a conversation with Alexandra. After all of those weeks in close company with her, Rebekah had failed to find they had much in common. Except Asher, of course.

"How are two of my favorite ladies this fine Sabbath morning?" Pastor Miller's cheerful voice welcomed them at the door to the church.

Aunt Dolly laughed. "You are quite the diplomat, Pastor Miller. I suppose that all of the ladies in Nashville are your favorites."

He beamed at them. "Only the ones who are or may become members of the church."

"How are you feeling today, Una?" Aunt Dolly directed her words to the short woman who was beginning to show signs of her pregnancy and who stood next to the pastor.

Rebekah peeked over her aunt's shoulder at the dark-haired, green-eyed beauty who stood with one hand on the small of her back. Rumor said she was from a wealthy family, but her face glowed with humility and love for others. She was a talented baker as well. While her husband ministered to people's souls, she soothed their taste buds with delicious homemade pies and cakes.

Una shook her head. "I tire before I can get through a day's work."

A pang of remorse hit Rebekah, and tears threatened to overwhelm her as she watched the pastor and his wife. She wanted to start her own family, but would her dream ever come true? It seemed everyone was moving forward except Asher and her. When had it all started to go wrong? Was it that night at the river, the night he had pushed her away? Or had it started in New Orleans when she caught him dancing with Alexandra Lewis?

Her mind went back to the day Asher had told her he was going to war. The time between then and today had changed both of them. He was no longer the boy who wanted to live the simple life.

"I hope your frown is not an indictment of my sermon."

"No. . .no, sir." Rebekah shook her head for emphasis. "I was thinking of something else entirely."

"Hmm, I'm not sure it's much better to learn my sermon

had so little effect that you've already forgotten it. It has always been my hope that God will use my sermons to make a difference in the congregation's lives, not be forgotten before they pass through the exit."

Aunt Dolly came to her rescue. "You must forgive my niece, Pastor. She is pining over her young man, who was apparently unable to attend this morning."

Maybe it would be better if no one tried to rescue her. Rebekah's cheeks burned, and she glanced down, unable to bear the sympathetic expressions of the pastor and his wife.

Pastor Miller reached for her hand, placing it in both of his. "Perhaps you will allow me to bring my wife to visit with you and your aunt this week."

Aunt Dolly raised her parasol to shade her face. "I have an even better idea. Why don't you and Mrs. Miller come by today for dinner? Rebekah and I would welcome your company."

"If you're sure it's no imposition. . ."

"I insist. Please say you'll come. I know Rebekah agrees, don't you?"

Rebekah looked at the earnest face of the pastor. She'd rather have had her dinner alone, but she knew her duty. She forced a smile to her face. "We'd love having you join us."

Pastor Miller helped them enter their carriage. "Then we would be delighted."

"Excellent. We'll look for you within the half hour."

As the carriage rumbled away, Aunt Dolly turned to her. "You may remove that grimace from your face, Rebekah."

"I thought I was smiling."

"If that's a smile, I would hate to see what your face looks like when you are in pain."

Rebekah dropped her gaze, ashamed of her sour disposition. What would Asher think if he could see her right now? But that was exactly the problem. Asher was nowhere around. And he'd apparently forgotten his promise to approach her pa as soon as he returned to Nashville. Well, she was not going to pine for him. She would smile and converse as if her heart were not breaking apart. What did it matter if everyone, even God, had abandoned her?

Aunt Dolly cleared her throat. "I have an idea I'd like to discuss with you, Rebekah."

The tone of her aunt's voice was light, but Rebekah twisted her gloves between her hands. Was her aunt about to chastise her for some other shortcoming? "Is something wrong?"

"Oh, no, dear. Not at all. But it is a rather delicate matter, and I am concerned that I may hurt your feelings."

Rebekah smiled brightly even as she steeled herself for yet another blow. "You could never do that, Dolly. Please tell me what's wrong."

"I was thinking about that weekend we spent at Mrs. Lewis's family home in Natchez."

Rebekah shifted on the seat. "I'd just as soon forget that weekend."

"I know, dear, but it made me think of that piano in the drawing room. I used to play it for my dear husband, but since his death, I simply don't have the heart for it." Aunt Dolly paused for a quick breath. "I was wondering about arranging piano lessons."

Piano lessons? What an intriguing idea. Her jaw muscles relaxed, allowing her smile to become more natural. "But wouldn't that be expensive?"

"I wouldn't have suggested it if I couldn't afford it."

A sudden scene flashed in Rebekah's mind. She and Asher were sitting on a piano bench, their shoulders touching as he turned the pages. Beautiful music was pouring from the piano as her fingers swept up and down the keyboard. Somewhere in the background, Alexandra wept into a handkerchief. . . .

"Rebekah? We're home, dear."

The carriage had stopped in front of Aunt Dolly's home.

Rebekah climbed down and followed her aunt inside, her feet practically dancing to the sweeping melody playing in her mind.

❧

Rebekah's fingers seemed to tangle as she tried to sort out the notes on the paper in front of her nose. She leaned forward and stared at the sheet, but the little black marks made no sense. Whoever thought to write down music in dots and slashes that had no relevance to the black and white keys under her fingers?

From behind her, the quick footsteps of Mr. Smothers, the piano teacher for many of the young ladies of Nashville, approached the stool. "Let's try again, shall we?"

His squeaky voice irritated her further, but Rebekah bit down on her lower lip. It wasn't Mr. Smothers's fault she had no talent. "It's hopeless. I cannot even master the simplest of tunes. I will never be able to play a real song." She twisted on the piano stool to face him.

Mr. Smothers pursed his lips, looking as if he had bitten into a crab apple. "Anyone can learn the basics, my dear. But you must apply yourself if you wish to excel. I believe the problem may be your advanced age. Most of my students are a great deal younger. Their fingers are likely more nimble and their minds not so cluttered with. . .with whatever it is that clutters your mind."

A knock on the front door interrupted them.

Rebekah pushed back the piano stool. "I think we've both suffered enough today."

Mr. Smothers did not have to look quite so relieved to be done with their lesson as he gathered his music sheets and overcoat. Rebekah saw him to the door, pondering whether or not to free the poor man from future trials by dispensing with his services. She would mention it to Aunt Dolly tonight. It was obvious she would never learn to play well, and there was no sense in spending Aunt Dolly's money for a lost cause.

They were met at the front door by Pastor and Mrs. Miller, who had dropped by for a visit. Much to her surprise, Rebecca had enjoyed having lunch with them after church last week. They seemed to find such joy in reaching out to the community, and their love for one another was evident in every glance they shared.

Rebekah trailed them into the parlor and sat in one corner, listening as they discussed the Indian attack at a settlement only a few miles north of Nashville. The people living there had not been killed, but their livestock was stolen, and several barns burned to the ground.

"Our wagons were stopped by a group of Indians on the Natchez Road." Aunt Dolly smiled at her. "But thanks to the quick thinking of my niece, we were able to come to an agreement to share our food with them and thus avoid disaster."

Una Miller shuddered, making her teacup teeter. "I fear for all of our lives if we cannot find a way to live together in Christian love."

Aunt Dolly passed a tray of pastries to her, but Rebekah could not concentrate on them enough to choose one. Her mind raced with questions. "How can the Indians practice Christian love if they don't even know Christ?"

Pastor Miller nodded. "That is an excellent question. Since coming to the frontier, Una and I have been burdened by our concern for these Indians, and we've prayed for God to show us how we might help them."

"Has God answered your prayers?" Rebekah asked.

"Indeed, I believe so." A smile of delight wreathed his face. "I think we were called to this area to found a school for the Indians. I understand an Indian couple has bought a farm about fifteen miles away. Una and I are planning a trip to visit them next week."

Rebekah listened as the pastor and his wife expounded on their ideas, but inside she felt they were taking on a task too great for two people. It would take more than one earnest couple to help the different Indian tribes adapt.

Her mind wandered to a recent newspaper article describing General Jackson's position on the Indian problem. His argument against the Indians seemed based on his belief that they could not live inside the sovereign territory of the United States. He proposed that those Indians who did not wish to become subject to American law should be moved to land outside the United States, land on the far side of the Mississippi River.

While she admired the general's bravery and military accomplishments and dearly loved his placid wife, she was appalled at his stance on the subject of Indians. It was too easy to put herself in the place of the Indians. Would she want to be told to leave her home just because someone with different beliefs had moved into the area?

". . .near your family, Rebekah. Would you like to join us?"

Rebekah's head jerked up. "I beg your pardon."

A frown from Aunt Dolly made Rebekah cringe inwardly. "I'm sure my niece would relish the chance to visit her family."

For the first time that afternoon, Rebekah felt a genuine spark of happiness. How wonderful it would be to see her family. "May I?"

Pastor Miller winked at her before turning to Aunt Dolly. "We'd love to have both of you join us."

"No, thank you." Aunt Dolly shuddered. "I find the country singularly depressing."

"If everyone thought as you and I, Nashville would be a very crowded place." Mrs. Miller laughed and rose to her feet, and her husband followed suit.

Rebekah practically bounced to her feet and trailed her aunt and their guests to the door. She could almost see her parents and siblings as they were reunited. Maybe she and Eleanor could even have a picnic under the shady leaves of the tulip poplar.

Pastor Miller adjusted his hat. "I will let you know the details in a day or two."

As soon as they closed the door on the Millers, Rebekah threw her arms around her aunt.

"My goodness. It seems someone is yearning for home." Aunt Dolly laughed. "If I didn't know better, I'd think you were unhappy here."

"Not at all. You are the sweetest aunt any girl could imagine, but I do miss home."

"I'm flattered." Aunt Dolly patted her cheek. "In the meantime, I will need your help with our ball."

All of Rebekah's excitement melted away like an early frost. She looked at her aunt in horror. "You're going to host a ball?"

❧

"Please, Lord, heal Asher's heart." Hot tears seared Rebekah's cheeks. She gripped her hands more tightly together and rested her aching head against the side of her bed. "You know how much I love him, but something seems to be terribly wrong between us. Should I stay here and wait for Asher to change into the man I once loved? Do I remain patient with him and pray for him? Or should I give up and go back home? Lord, it was so much better back then. Maybe if I go back home, we can rediscover the love we once had. Please, Lord, show me what to do."

Rebekah ended her prayer and climbed into bed. She was not looking forward to tomorrow evening's ball. But once it was over, there would be no real reason for her to stay in Nashville. Aunt Dolly no longer needed her assistance. In fact, she had very little to do with herself during the day, especially since she had convinced Aunt Dolly to cancel her music lessons.

Every day, she hoped Asher would come by and tell her he'd been out to ask Pa for her hand in marriage. Every time the knocker sounded on the front door, her hopes had risen along with her heartbeat—and every time, she was disappointed. The only time she saw Asher was a social occasion. Never alone.

She turned over and sighed. She no longer paid much attention to the sounds of the city outside her window, but she would gladly exchange them for the melodic song of crickets and bullfrogs. More tears slipped free of her eyes and dampened the pillow beneath her head. What if God didn't send her an answer she could understand?

Rebekah closed her eyes, but sleep would not come. She slipped out of bed once again and returned to her knees. No words formed in her mind as she tried to pray, but a feeling of love and comfort enveloped her. The tears stopped, and she could feel a smile turning up the corners of her mouth. This was the touch of the Lord. She knew it deep in her heart. No matter how things worked out with Asher, Jesus would always love her.

eleven

"But I don't want to be a teller." Asher's voice had risen in volume as he tried to explain to his pa why he wanted to continue working for the militia. His parents were frustrated with his refusal to change his mind, but he was equally frustrated with their inability to grasp his desire to launch a challenging, interesting career that would keep him in close contact with General Jackson. They wanted him to embrace a boring future with a steady income that offered no chance for fame or fortune. They did not understand the importance of what he was involved in.

"It makes a lot more sense than hanging around that braggart, Colonel Lewis." His pa took a deep breath and released it with a grunt. "You are letting that man draw you into questionable schemes without a thought to the consequences."

"It's not like that, Pa."

"Then tell me what it is like." Pa's eyes narrowed. Asher could almost feel the flashes of lightning coming from them.

He hated arguing with his pa, but this was too important an issue. The way to convince his parents was through calm and rational discussion. He tamped down his anger. "I cannot. I've sworn an oath."

"To whom? The United States Army or to that New Orleans fop?"

"Pa, I've never heard you cast such aspersions. Colonel Lewis is a respected officer in General Jackson's militia."

"Isn't he the one you report to? Or do you have another reason for spending so much time at the Lewis home?"

Asher could feel his anger building again. First Rebekah and now his own family. Didn't anyone trust him anymore? "What kind of son do you think you raised?" He turned away and looked out the window.

After a moment, he felt Pa's hand on his shoulder. "I'm sorry. You're right. Your ma and I raised you to be an honest, God-fearing man. We have to allow you to make your own decisions."

Asher wanted to turn around, but he could not. It was time for his family to realize that he was fully grown. Maybe when he and Rebekah got married. . .as soon as he asked Mr. Taylor for permission to propose. And why was he taking so long to do that?

Somewhere along their journey from New Orleans, Rebekah had changed. He hardly knew her anymore. At first he'd thought she was worried about her aunt or maybe overtired from the hardships of traveling, but they'd been back in Nashville for nearly a month and there had been plenty of time for her to recover. Mrs. Quinn seemed to be thriving, so that wasn't the problem.

He was beginning to think Rebekah didn't love him anymore. She was distant and cold the one time he called on her. Of course, the reason he hadn't been by more often was because he was busy preparing for their future. But had she understood that? No. Instead of being glad to see him, she seemed to be waiting for him to make some confession of wrongdoing. Asher never knew what to say anymore to bring a smile to her face. It was impossible to talk to her about anything other than the weather or her aunt's health. What had happened to the sweet girl he'd fallen in love with?

He felt Pa's hand fall away and listened as retreating footsteps indicated that he had given up.

Asher wanted to bridge the gap between them, but he had no idea how to do that. At one time he would have talked to

Rebekah about his quandary, but now that option seemed out of the question. His sister was available to listen, but he didn't want to draw her into the middle of this. She would feel torn between her loyalty to her parents and her love for her big brother.

He pulled his watch from the front pocket of his waistcoat and popped it open. It was nearly time to leave for tonight's ball. He had promised Alexandra he would attend to help ease her introduction to local society. . .even though he doubted she would have any trouble. But perhaps she could give him some sage advice. Women always seemed to understand these things better than men.

☙

Rebekah put a hand on the balustrade and slowly descended the staircase. How different things looked since that long-ago afternoon when she and Pa had first arrived at Aunt Dolly's house. Gone were the grime and disarray that had greeted them that day. The whole house literally sparkled this evening, with dozens of candles lending a warm glow to the staircase and entry hall. Harriet and the maids had done an impeccable job getting the house ready for tonight's ball.

The afternoon Rebekah had learned Aunt Dolly planned a soiree in her niece's honor, she had been appalled. She felt so uncomfortable in social settings. All of those parties in New Orleans had been difficult because she had so little in common with most of the people who attended. And then the debacle at Tanner Plantation. . . It was enough to make a person want to avoid society for the next twenty years or so.

After her initial response, however, Rebekah had been unable to withstand her aunt's obvious desire to throw a party. And she had to admit the planning had been fun—the invitations, menus, and decorating. But now, half the city would be coming to judge whether or not she was a worthy relative of her dashing aunt.

Something smelled delicious. The new cook Aunt Dolly had hired was outdoing herself for tonight's event. The aromas of roasted meat and zesty sauces made her mouth water.

"You look absolutely stunning." Aunt Dolly's voice floated up from the foot of the stairs. Rebekah thought her aunt was the one who looked stunning in a brand-new aqua gown that enhanced her natural beauty.

"You're the real reason everyone's coming. All of your friends are anxious to see you again now that you've fully recovered your health. I doubt anyone will even notice me, which is a perfectly acceptable state of affairs."

Aunt Dolly wagged her finger at Rebekah. "You'll be turning heads and collecting compliments from all of the eligible men. Especially a certain dashing young captain."

Rebekah felt her smile fading away. If only that were true. But Asher had been so distant since they'd returned. Was he regretting his promise to her? Did he yearn for a more sophisticated wife? Someone with all the accomplishments of a lady? Someone named Alexandra?

She shook her head in an attempt to silence the needling suggestion. But the evidence was overwhelming. Whenever she tried to find out why Asher was distracted, he pushed away her concern. Something elemental had changed in him. He was as charming as ever but. . .

Tears stung her eyes. Rebekah missed those quiet afternoons back home, sitting under the shade of "their" tulip poplar while they made endless plans for a future together. A future that seemed more distant now than ever before.

Rebekah had wondered if she should stay in Nashville and wait for Asher to reaffirm he still wished to marry her as he had promised that night at Tanner Plantation. How well she remembered his assurance that he would approach her pa the very first day they returned. Yet the first day had become the first week. And then two weeks. Now it was nearly a month since their return, but Asher had made absolutely no mention of asking for her hand in marriage.

There was no getting around it. After the tearful hours she had spent last night on her knees talking to God about her dreams, hopes, and fears, Rebekah felt she could not ignore the tug on her heart. There was only one thing to do. She loved Asher more than life itself, and she did not want him to feel trapped by the promise he obviously regretted making.

Tonight she would release him. She was determined to do the right thing and tell Asher he was free to pursue others. His feelings for her must have faded. He would be happier if she told him he was free to move on without her.

A knock on the door indicated the arrival of the first guests. As predicted, they laughed and chatted with Aunt Dolly and paid Rebekah very little attention before moving to the ballroom. Soon the steady stream of townspeople made it clear the ball was going to be a success—in sheer numbers of attendees if nothing else.

Alexandra and her parents arrived, gushing over Aunt Dolly's house and complimenting her on the large number of people attending her party.

Rebekah breathed a sigh of relief when they moved on.

The next group entering brought a genuine smile to her face as they included some of her favorite people in Nashville—Rachel Jackson, Pastor and Mrs. Miller, and Mr. and Mrs. Landon, Asher's parents. Asher, however, was conspicuously absent in spite of the fact he had accepted Aunt Dolly's invitation.

Rebekah stood beside her aunt and greeted the arriving townspeople for two more hours and wondered why she had ever agreed to a party. She had smiled for so long that her mouth actually hurt. And her feet. She should have worn her sensible day shoes. But they would not have complemented her new periwinkle blue gown, so she had sacrificed comfort for appearance. But what good would her sacrifice do if she were crippled from wearing the high-heeled brocade shoes dyed to match her dress?

"You're the most beautiful girl in the whole of Nashville." Asher's voice pulled her from her thoughts.

Her heart fluttered when she looked up and saw his face. He was the man she would always love. "Asher." Her heart raced so that she barely forced the word out.

He bowed over her hand and straightened. "I've missed you so much. It's hard not getting to see you every day. I almost wish we were back on the Natchez Road so I could talk to you all day long."

She studied his face. Was it her imagination, or did Asher look tired this evening? There were dark circles under his eyes and lines on either side of his mouth. It made her want to draw his head down and stroke his hair until he was rested.

"I would like to see you alone before the evening is over, Rebekah. There's something very exciting I want to tell you about."

She searched his face for a hint of what he meant. Had he been out to the farm as he'd promised? Was all of her soul-searching for naught? And if he had secured her parents' blessing, was that enough proof that he truly loved her and only her?

But what if she was jumping to conclusions again? Wasn't this exactly what Asher had said to her the day he'd announced he was going to war? That he had "something" to tell her? Why should she assume that his idea of good news would match hers? It certainly had not all those months ago. Besides, she had already made her decision, hadn't she?

"Just a moment." Rebekah turned to her aunt and hesitated. She was very aware of Asher watching her, so she chose her words with care. "Would it be permissible if I step away for a few minutes?"

"Go on, Rebekah." Aunt Dolly took Rebekah's hand and placed it on Asher's arm. "I'll stay here and greet any late guests. You two can stand right down there at the door to the parlor. That way you can have some privacy and still satisfy propriety."

Rebekah allowed Asher to draw her away from the entry hall. "What do you have to tell me?"

"It's the best of good fortune! Pa has been trying to coerce me into taking a job at the bank, but I cannot see myself working in a dingy office for the rest of my life. Now that the war is over, Colonel Lewis has secured me a position working directly for General Jackson. His popularity has only continued to grow since the victory in New Orleans. I believe he's a man destined for great things, and as a key member of his staff, I will have the chance to be part of them."

She looked at the crisp coat of his uniform. No words would form in her mind.

"Don't you understand what this means? I'll soon be making enough money to buy us a home. We'll finally be able to make our dreams come true."

Rebekah could not bear to hear any more excuses from him. "I'm going home."

"What! What do you mean?"

"Pastor and Mrs. Miller are going out to the country to visit, and I'm going with them." She looked at the wall behind his shoulder. "I may not come back."

"What are you talking about?"

Rebekah wanted to pour out her heart to him, but she could not. He was not the same man who had once shared her dreams and helped her solve her problems. He had become a stranger. She closed her eyes for a moment and sent a prayer heavenward for the right words. "I think we need some time apart."

Asher shook his head slowly. "Haven't we had enough time apart?"

"I. . .Asher, I don't know what to say or think. You seem reluctant to speak to—"

"I'm not reluctant. I've been busy. A lot has happened since we got back from New Orleans."

Rebekah sighed. She was so tired of hearing his empty excuses.

"What do you want me to do?" His brows drew together. "Do you want me to resign from the militia and take a job in the bank like my pa?"

"I don't care what profession you choose."

His frown eased a little. "I'm glad to hear that. Please be patient, Rebekah. Soon you'll have the whole city at your feet."

He still didn't understand her. A tear escaped from the corner of her eye. "I don't want the whole city."

"Exactly what do you want then?"

She looked at him, longing to touch him. "I want a man who is eager to marry me, not one who feels trapped by a promise he made when he was an idealistic youngster."

He put his hands on her shoulders. "Rebekah, don't be preposterous."

She twisted away and moved back into the hall, her heart breaking as his words and tone showed how little he valued her feelings. Didn't he realize how long she had agonized over this? "It may be preposterous to you, but you asked what I want, and I have told you."

"I should have known this would happen." Asher's mouth became a straight slash and his eyes hardened. "You are becoming quite adept at manipulating people."

Rebekah's head jerked as if he had slapped her. She doubted she could have been hurt more by a physical blow. "I think you should go now, Captain Landon."

"If that's what you *want*."

His emphasis on the word made her cringe, but she didn't try to defend herself.

Asher pulled a pair of snowy white gloves from the belt of his uniform and jammed his fingers into them. "Don't think this scheme of yours has me fooled. I love you, Rebekah, and I want to marry you. But I have too much respect for you to rush into a marriage when I don't know if I can support you."

He left her standing at the parlor door, her heart lying in pieces around her fancy shoes. She lifted a hand as if to stop him but let it fall to her side. What more could she say?

☙

Asher stalked away from Rebekah, wondering if he shouldn't leave Mrs. Quinn's home right away. But his parents would be disappointed if he did not make at least a brief appearance. A pang of remorse pierced his anger as he thought of the scene with his pa earlier. He needed to put the argument with Rebekah aside for right now.

Pa had taken the news of his decision to work with Colonel Lewis hard. Asher did not like hurting his pa, but this was *his* life, and he had to make his own way to success. Everything he'd dreamed of was within his grasp. Well, almost everything.

Asher stopped for a moment and concentrated on taking deep breaths. He would not allow Rebekah's immaturity to spoil his evening. When had she become so. . .he searched for the right word. . .so *backward*? Why had she set her heart on living way out in the wilderness? He might understand her feelings if she had not been living in Nashville for more than a year. But she had experienced the luxuries of town life. It made no sense to shun progress.

She must know how much he liked the hustle and bustle of city life. Years ago, he and his family had left behind the dull and thankless world of farming. He was no longer the type to break his back to provide the bare necessities for his wife and children. There were so many more opportunities here for a man to make his mark on the world. Why couldn't Rebekah see that?

He pulled his gloves off and tucked them into his belt. Nobody was going to stop him from succeeding.

He stepped into the ballroom and looked around. The orchestra was playing, and several couples were swaying in the center of the room while other guests lined the walls, spreading the latest gossip and showing off their fancy clothes.

He spotted Alexandra across the room. Her warm smile was like a balm to his lacerated heart. He eased his way through the crowd. Why couldn't Rebekah be more like her, pleasant and welcoming? Alexandra didn't seem to think he was deficient in some ridiculous way. She accepted him for the man he was.

"Bonju, Captain." She pulled out her fan and fluttered it in front of her face. "Congratulations! Papa told me of your new position."

Asher bowed. "I am flattered to be selected."

"You need not feel flattered, Captain. Papa is lucky to be able to rely on your strength and intelligence. The general keeps him so busy he barely has time to eat a meal with his family."

A hand fell on his shoulder, and Asher turned to see Colonel Lewis. "Sir, we were just talking about you."

The man looked from Asher to his daughter, his bushy eyebrows climbing toward his hairline. "In my day, there were other topics more interesting for a young couple to discuss than work and parents."

Alexandra's cheeks brightened to the hue of a summer sunrise. "Papa!"

Even though the colonel had made several comments during their journey from New Orleans about a suitable match for his daughter, Asher had always brushed aside his rather clumsy hints.

But tonight was different. Tonight he was seeing things with greater clarity. "Don't be embarrassed," he told Alexandra. "If I had as pretty a daughter as you, I would be equally surprised."

She tapped his arm with the end of her fan. "You are quite a smooth talker, sir."

"It is nothing but the truth, Miss Lewis." He bowed slightly. "May I have this dance?"

"That's more like it." Colonel Lewis beamed at them. "Don't let one of these other Nashville beaus turn her head. I happen to know that Alexandra thinks you are quite the dashing war hero."

Asher drew her onto the dance floor before the colonel could embarrass them further.

She curtsied, her gaze on the floor.

Asher took her hand as they followed the dance steps. "Don't worry. Parents have a decided talent when it comes to discomfiting their children." He nodded his head toward his own parents who were watching them circle the dance floor. "They are probably talking about us right now."

She glanced toward them and then at him. "What do you think they're saying?"

"What else but that I am the luckiest man here to have such a beautiful young lady as my dance partner?"

Alexandra's smile rewarded him. "Thank you for your sweet compliments. Since we arrived in Nashville, not everyone has been so welcoming."

Now this was more like it. More like what he had expected the evening to hold. Pleasant company and gentle flirting rather than accusations and manipulative ultimatums. "The young ladies are probably jealous to have such a sophisticated newcomer competing for the attention of our local men."

Her hand squeezed his. "Me. . .sophisticated? But I

was raised on a plantation. Surely the ladies here have the advantage since they have grown up in the center of Nashville. I am very much the outsider."

Asher looked to the doorway in time to see Rebekah entering. Good. Let her see exactly how much it would affect him if she left Nashville. He returned his attention to his dance partner. "But you have something none of them have."

"What is that?"

"You have an air of mystery and intrigue. None of the local gents knew you before you attained the full flower of your beauty." He nodded at a tall, graceful blond dancing a few yards away. "You would never think it to look at her tonight, but I remember when Dorcas Montgomery was as thin as a sapling and more clumsy than a newborn colt."

Alexandra was so easy to talk to, and he had only to look at her expression to realize that she did seem to admire him. He ignored the whispery voice of his conscience. Alexandra was only being friendly, and there was nothing wrong with letting her kindness soothe his bruised heart.

twelve

"Watch out for that rut." Una Miller, perched next to her husband, pointed toward the road. "I'm sure Rebekah is tired of being bounced around."

If she had not been taught better, Rebekah would have voiced her agreement. She was beginning to wish Pastor Miller was driving Pa's wagon. It was a bit disturbing to be pitched about when they were sitting so high above the ground. But at least she was going home.

Away from Asher. Away from heartache.

Yet when she considered a future without him, Rebekah wondered if there would ever be joy in her life again. She only knew she could not stand to watch him dance and flirt with Alexandra.

Anxious to drive the uncomfortable pictures from her mind, she leaned forward. "Thank you so much for letting me come with you."

Pastor Miller's hands slackened on the reins as he glanced back at her, causing the buggy to increase its speed. "You've already thanked us three times."

"We've been planning this visit for weeks," his wife added. "Having your company only adds to our pleasure."

Rebekah's stomach clenched as the landscape rushed past them. Would it be rude to ask Pastor Miller to slow down a bit? Although she was anxious to reach her parents' home, she had no wish to risk life and limb in the process. She leaned back to escape the dizzying sensation, but it was no use. Even closing her eyes did no good.

"I promise Roman is a very competent driver."

Her eyelids flew open and a blush heated Rebekah's cheeks. "I'm sure he is. It's a bit disconcerting though. We must be covering more than a mile every ten minutes."

When the pastor looked back over his shoulder once again, she wanted to beg him to keep his attention fixed on the road. Perhaps she should ask the couple about something that had been bothering her for a while. "Will there be Indians in heaven?"

Pastor Miller's hands jerked convulsively on the reins, slowing the buggy considerably. "Of course there will be."

Mrs. Miller turned in her seat, and Rebekah saw a hint of tears in her eyes. "We are concerned all the time about those who have had no chance to ask Jesus into their hearts. It's our hope and prayer that all men will soon heed the words of our Lord and choose everlasting life."

Rebekah leaned forward again. "What about those people who don't believe the Indians can be forgiven?"

This time, Pastor Miller answered her question. "We are all people in the eyes of God, and we have all sinned and need a Savior. Including me. Whether it's killing or stealing or even telling a lie about someone."

"I know, Pastor. 'For all have sinned, and come short of the glory of God.'"

"That's right." Mrs. Miller's pink bonnet moved up and down as she nodded. "But don't forget the next verse in Romans: 'Being justified freely by his grace through the redemption that is in Christ Jesus.' The Bible promises that anyone, not just this group or that one, can be saved."

"How will the Indians get to know about Jesus?" Rebekah's fear of the buggy ride began to subside. "Pa and Ma always read to us from the Bible when I was growing up. And we'd get to hear sermons from traveling preachers who stayed over and preached in the little church Pa and some of the other men built. But who preaches to the Indians?"

"That's exactly why we want to start a school," Mrs. Miller answered. "We feel the Lord wants us to share His message with them."

Rebekah played with the strings of her bonnet. "Remember when Aunt Dolly told you about the Indians who stopped us on the Natchez Road?"

She waited for them to nod before continuing. "There was one Indian, a boy really, who made me stop and wonder about what future he had."

Pastor Miller tossed a smile at her over his shoulder. "There's no telling what ramifications your decision to share your food may have had. A light shower falls and, when joined by other rains, becomes a flood that carries everything before it."

Rebekah felt another stirring of the excitement that had gripped her the day they met the Indians. A whisper echoed through her mind. Was it a sign? Was she meant to do something about teaching the Indians? But what did she know about such things?

A movement caught her attention, and Rebekah shaded her eyes, straining to see who it was. Had their conversation brought Indians down on them? The harder she looked, however, the more familiar the figure seemed. She watched him raise an arm up and swing down on what looked like a fence post. His head raised, and she recognized him. "Pa! It's Pa! Please stop!"

Pastor Miller pulled up on the reins, and Rebekah scrambled past the Millers, heedless of the great height that had terrified her earlier. She was home!

"Pa!" she yelled as loudly as she could and had the satisfaction of seeing the man's head turn toward her. She barely noticed the second figure, who'd been hidden until her pa turned. All she could really see was Pa's familiar face. She ran across the wide field and was caught up in his arms and swung around like a girl of four instead of the young lady she was supposed to be.

"My Becka." He hugged her as tight as a corset bone and kissed her on the cheek before setting her back on her feet. "Aren't you a sight!"

His smile was as warm as summer sunshine. It melted the lump she'd been carrying in her chest since the argument with Asher. She was home, and everything was going to be all right.

"I want you to meet someone very special, Becka." He turned to the man who had been helping him mend fence posts. This is our new neighbor, Wohali. He owns the land we're standing on."

Her eyes widened as Rebekah took in the stranger's long, black hair, dark eyes, and swarthy skin. An Indian! This must be the man the Millers had come to meet. But why was Pa working with him? If the ground had opened up underneath her feet, she could not have been more surprised. No matter what else changed in her life, she'd clung to the belief that everything at home would remain the same. How unsettling to find even bigger changes here than in Nashville. "How do you do?"

The tall man nodded his head. "I am pleased to meet you."

Would wonders never cease? Not only was the Indian a landowner, his grammar and diction were impeccable. She realized her mouth had dropped open, and she shut it with an audible *pop*.

"Now it's your turn." Her pa nodded toward the Millers, who were waiting in their buggy.

Rebekah, Wohali, and Pa made their way across the field toward the road, and she performed the introductions.

"Why don't you go on up to the house with the Millers? Wohali and I will be there in a few minutes. I don't want to waste a minute of your visit." Pa turned to the pastor. "I hope you can stay overnight with us so we'll have more time to hear all about Rebekah's adventures before she returns to Nashville."

"I'm not going back, Pa." The lump returned, larger than before. She turned away to hide the tears that had sprung to her eyes.

"I see." He squeezed her shoulder gently. "We'll talk about it at home. Your ma and your siblings are going to be thrilled to see you."

Rebekah blinked her eyes rapidly to force the tears back. She did not know if she could talk about her feelings. Better to remain silent and stoic. She concentrated on climbing safely into the buggy as her vision blurred.

❧

"Hurry up, Rebekah. We're going to be late for church." Eleanor was practically jumping up and down in her impatience.

"What do you mean? There's plenty of time to get to the church before the service begins."

Ma unpinned her apron and folded it neatly before placing it on the kitchen shelf. "Your sister is right, Rebekah."

"What? We've never left for church this early."

Ma sighed. "Eleanor, go get your brother. Rebekah, sit down. There are a few things we need to discuss."

When Eleanor left the cabin, Rebekah looked toward her ma with some apprehension. Was this yet another change? Since coming home last week, she had discovered many things were different than she remembered. Of course, she expected Eleanor and Donny to be more grown up, but so much else had changed. Ma looked older, her brown hair liberally streaked with gray. And Pa, who once prided himself on his independence, was working with Wohali nearly every day.

Even the crops had changed. Pa still planted corn, but he also had several acres of wheat. Here at home, he and Ma had added an extra bedroom so she and Eleanor would no longer have to sleep in the loft. Although she knew the changes were indications of progress and prosperity, Rebekah would have much preferred that everything stay the same.

"There have been some who are not happy about Wohali and his family moving into our community."

Rebekah nodded. She did not personally mind having Indians for neighbors, but her imagination boggled at the idea of Wohali's wife joining a quilting bee or exchanging recipes with the ladies in the area.

"Your pa and I have prayed about the tense situation since they moved here, and we believe we received an answer when Wohali asked whether or not he and Noya—that's his wife, who has become a dear friend—could attend our church. We decided we would help them get established by escorting them for the first few Sundays."

"Why didn't he go to the preacher?"

Ma smiled and patted her hand. "We've grown fairly close to Wohali and Noya. I guess they feel more comfortable talking to your pa than some stranger down the road."

Someone, probably Pa, had brought in a handful of wildflowers and laid them on a cloth in the center of the table. Rebekah picked one up and twirled it between her fingers. "How did they come to buy their place?"

"Wohali was educated by a missionary who came to share the gospel with his tribe. He's a Christian and very eager to be a part of our community. It took a long time, but he and his wife managed to save enough money to buy some land."

"They left their tribe?"

Ma placed a calming hand over Rebekah's fingers to keep her from destroying the delicate wildflower. "I'm sure it was a difficult choice, but Noya told me they prayed for guidance and were led to move away."

The front door swung inward, and Pa stepped inside. "Are my girls ready to get going?"

"I'll just be a minute." Rebekah hurried into the bedroom and rummaged through her bags to find her hairpins before twisting her braid into a knot and quickly pinning it into place. What an amazing story. She was glad God didn't expect her to leave her home. . .or did He?

Her hands fell to her sides as a sudden question struck her. All the times she and Asher had planned for their future, it had never occurred to her to pray for God's guidance. She had prayed for an answer before she broke things off with him last week. But had she prayed for His will, or had she only prayed for her own plans to be fulfilled?

❧

Asher wiped his hands against his dress trousers and watched for the Taylors to arrive in their buckboard. He greeted his former neighbors, many of whom wanted to hear of his exploits with the Tennessee militia. He was well into describing General Jackson's canny strategies when he realized that none of the men were paying him any attention. They had all turned to look at the latest arrivals.

Asher turned to see what had caused the commotion, and his eyes nearly jumped from his head. Rebekah and her family were pulling up to the church—with a couple of Indians on their buckboard.

One of the men who had been standing in front of Asher grabbed his wife and escorted her back to their wagon. Another was pulled away by his wife and into the church. A third man spat at the ground and rubbed a suggestive thumb on his holster.

Asher wondered what he should do. Ignore the Taylors? But that was why he had made the trip out here. He wanted to patch things up between him and Rebekah. Now that a few days had passed, surely she had begun to see reason.

He stepped forward. "Mr. and Mrs. Taylor. It's nice to see you this fine Sabbath day."

"Hello, Asher." The older man did not smile, and Asher wondered if Rebekah had mentioned their argument.

Mrs. Taylor, however, smiled broadly at him and put her hand on his arm. "What a lovely surprise. Rebekah did not tell us you might visit today. I hope you will stay for dinner. We are having our new neighbors over, also."

Asher assumed a pleasant expression as she introduced Wohali and Noya. The man's posture reminded him of a large cat, sleek and dangerous, a formidable adversary. He inclined his head in a slight nod. "How did you come to meet the Taylors?"

"They are our neighbors." The dark-skinned man nodded at Mr. Taylor. "We work well together. What one man cannot accomplish, two often can."

Asher could not argue that logic. "I'm sure Mr. Taylor and his family are happy to have you living so close by."

Wohali described the work he and Rebekah's pa had accomplished over the past season. Asher was impressed. Not only was the Indian articulate, he was obviously a hard worker and interested in making a comfortable home for his family. Just like Asher wanted to do. With Rebekah. For a moment he felt the pull to move back out here and farm. But what was he thinking? He was much better suited to work in Nashville.

He followed the Taylors into the little church, his mind in a whirl. It was hard to pay attention to the pastor's sermon about Jesus' warning to store treasures in heaven.

The church felt warm, and Asher found himself sliding down in the pew. He cleared his throat and pulled himself upright. It would not do for these people to see him sleeping in a public place, especially in a church. He was going to have to learn better discipline if he was going to keep his position with General Jackson.

He tried to catch Rebekah's attention, but she was totally

engrossed in the sermon, following along in her Bible and nodding as the pastor described the pitfalls of focusing on wealth and position. Asher didn't see why good Christians couldn't have those things. The Bible didn't say that one had to be poor and miserable to make it into heaven.

Finally, the service ended. Everyone stood and sang an invitational hymn.

Asher half expected the Indian couple to approach the pulpit, but they didn't. In fact, the whole morning seemed to have been wasted.

Somehow he ended up escorting Eleanor out to the front of the church instead of Rebekah. She let go of his arm the minute they stepped outside, dashing off to say hello to some of the other young people from the area.

He looked around and caught sight of Rebekah standing near her pa's wagon. He hurried over and offered her a hand, relieved when she accepted it. "It's good to see you looking so well, Rebekah. I don't have much time—I have to be back in Nashville this afternoon for a meeting—but I wanted to tell you that I'm sorry about our. . .discussion. . .the other night." He also wanted to tell her how much he missed her, but they only had a few seconds before the older adults would reach the wagon. "Please forgive me."

"Of course I forgive you, Asher." She said the words he wanted to hear, but Asher could see from her expression that something was still wrong. He wanted to say something more, but there wasn't enough time. Her parents had nearly reached the wagon.

He made his excuses to the Taylors and climbed back on his horse, wondering if he had accomplished anything by coming all this way.

❧

Rebekah ignored the teasing of her younger sister on the way home. Eleanor simply didn't understand the situation. She was full of romantic notions, exactly as Rebekah had been at her age.

Whether she should marry Asher was a matter of faith, not romance. If she and Asher were going to repair their relationship, they would have to spend more than a few seconds talking about their problems. She could not withhold forgiveness—the Lord's Prayer said Christians should forgive others if they wanted to be forgiven for their own transgressions. But forgiveness was one thing. Deciding what to do about marriage was another thing entirely.

Rebekah could tell that Asher had not changed much, if at all, since she'd come home. He apparently thought that an apology was sufficient to bridge the distance between them. She knew better.

Somehow she felt older than Asher now, more mature. While he was still chasing ephemeral dreams of wealth and fame, she had come to realize what was important in life. A sigh filled her, and Rebekah's heart ached for Asher to return to the Lord. All she could do was continue to pray that he would allow God to change his heart.

They dropped Wohali and Noya off at their home and continued to the cabin.

"You seem awfully quiet for a beautiful Sunday morning." Ma patted her knee. "Did you and Asher have time to talk?"

Rebekah shook her head.

Pa pulled up to let everyone off at the front door to the cabin. "Perhaps we can remedy that. Wohali mentioned that he and Noya need to get some things in Nashville, and I was thinking of going along with him. You can join us, Rebekah. I'm sure Noya would appreciate some feminine company."

"But shouldn't we all go?" Rebekah asked.

Ma laughed. "Didn't you notice how crowded it was with all of us in the wagon? I think I can wait until another time. And I have the feeling you need to work out some problems."

She put an arm around Rebekah and squeezed her tightly. "Hiding out here with your family is no way to resolve whatever it is that stands between you and Asher."

While Rebekah agreed with her mother, she wasn't sure if anything could bridge the widening rift between her and the man she had once shared future dreams with.

thirteen

Asher hated the waiting that seemed to go along with his new position as special liaison for Colonel Lewis. For nearly two weeks, he'd been expecting a directive from General Jackson. He'd been thrilled to finally receive a note from Colonel Lewis instructing him to attend a meeting in his home.

He pulled out his watch and glanced at it. He'd been alone in the colonel's study for nearly an hour. What could be keeping the man? His bored gaze again traveled around the handsomely appointed room. The luxurious furnishings testified to the importance of the Lewis family—deeply padded leather armchairs, a huge mahogany desk, and heavy drapes the color of a dark forest. One wall was lined with floor-to-ceiling shelves, partially filled with leather-clad books.

He'd spent at least fifteen minutes looking at the pristine volumes. The colonel took great care when he was perusing his books, just as he did with everything he was involved with—obviously one of the many reasons he had all the right connections.

A clock in the hallway chimed two more quarter hours. Asher was beginning to wonder if his host would ever appear when the door finally opened.

The colonel trundled across the room and gave him a perfunctory handshake. "Sorry to keep you waiting."

"I was wondering if I had the wrong time. . . ."

"Oh, no, no. I was up late last night escorting my ladies to the Purnell ball. They have to go to all of the parties, you know."

Asher noticed the man did look tired. His coat was creased

and dusty. His mustache, usually waxed and shaped into an upward curve, had drooped until it brushed his chin.

"And then it was up early again for an emergency meeting with General Jackson," the colonel continued. "I barely had time to get a note to you before I had to go right back out for yet another conference—this time with the local politicos. These Indians. . .I don't know what the general's going to do about them. I've been encouraging him to go forth with his removal plans even if those idiots in Washington haven't given him their blessing. What are they going to do to the Hero of New Orleans?"

Asher didn't know how he felt about the issue of Indian removal. While it seemed heartless to force them to leave their homes, it was equally obvious the quarrelsome Indians would never peacefully accept the land-hungry white settlers who arrived every week. However, he knew what response the colonel expected to hear. "Probably give him another medal when they realize he's single-handedly solved all of their problems."

The colonel slapped his back. "Exactly. Have a seat, boy." He walked to the far side of the polished mahogany desk in the center of the study.

Asher hesitated for a moment before taking one of the armchairs in front of the desk.

"I invited you here to ask for your help with a rather—"

The door swung open with a loud *thump*, and Alexandra hurried inside, her attention on the wall of books to Asher's right.

Asher jumped up and bowed to her. "Good afternoon, Miss Lewis."

"Captain Landon, what a pleasure." An eager smile lit her face.

Her father rose more slowly. "I'm holding an important meeting."

"Excuse me, Papa. I didn't realize you and Captain Landon were here."

Her smile should not have suggested duplicity, but Asher wondered if she was as unaware of his presence as she claimed. He could not help being a little flattered that she would risk her father's censure for a chance to see him. If only Rebekah was as anxious to spend time with him.

"I am so sorry to disturb you. I promised Mama that I would find the collection of William Shakespeare's sonnets."

Asher stepped toward her. "Perhaps I can help you find the volume you need."

Colonel Lewis sighed. "I guess we can postpone our meeting for a while, daughter. After the amount of time I've had this young man waiting, I imagine he could use some refreshment"—he winked at Asher—"and some refreshing company, too, eh?"

While Asher and Alexandra looked for the elusive volume, the colonel rang for refreshments. After a few minutes, a tall, slender slave brought in a silver tea service and quietly disappeared.

Alexandra took the seat next to Asher's and poured for the gentlemen, prattling on about how different things were out in the frontier than what she had seen in New Orleans. As she talked, she waved a lacy fan in front of her face. It was warm enough that Asher wished she would waft a breeze in his direction.

A noise from the far side of the desk turned his attention to the colonel.

After lowering his hand from attempting to cover his yawn, Colonel Lewis apologized. "Please forgive me. I guess the long working hours are catching up with me."

Alexandra put the tip of her fan against her bottom lip. "Staying out so late hasn't helped either, Papa. I woke up sometime during the night as I was a bit warm. I got up to open my window and saw you riding up—"

"Well, Captain Landon doesn't want to hear unimportant details about work. I guess I should just go upstairs and take a nap. Asher, could we finish our business at another time?"

"No problem, sir." Asher put his napkin on the tea tray and stood. "I shall take my leave."

"Please don't." Alexandra put a hand on his arm. "We can go down to the parlor. There's something I need to ask you about."

Asher raised an eyebrow. "Wouldn't it be more seemly to remain here?"

"Don't be ridiculous." She slid her hand under his elbow and pulled him into the hall. "No one will think a thing of it. You're like the big brother I always wanted. I truly value your opinion."

Asher allowed her to pull him to the parlor but stopped her from closing the door. It would be disastrous for them to be found closeted alone. Both their reputations would be in shambles.

"I saw Rebekah in Nashville yesterday."

Her words wiped out other considerations. If Rebekah was back in Nashville, it could only mean one thing—she was over their tiff. "I thought she would be back soon."

Alexandra's eyes narrowed. "And did you know she was in the company of an Indian couple?"

Surprise stiffened his back. But then the explanation dawned on him. They must be her Indian neighbors. Probably her whole family had come to Nashville, and she had agreed to escort the couple around since she would be the most familiar with Nashville. What a thoughtful deed. But he would have to remember to tell her to be careful. Not everyone would be so generous toward Indians, regardless of their aspirations.

"I didn't know what to say. Mama and Papa do not like the

uppity ways of some of the local Cherokees. They say that by befriending them we are only asking for trouble. The Indians are wild heathens with no idea in their heads but to stop us in any way they can."

Asher had to agree with that sentiment. The Indians he'd seen while serving under General Jackson had been bloodthirsty and dangerous. Of course, the same could be said of some of the soldiers. But the couple he'd met a few days ago at the Taylors' farm had seemed different. They had been well-spoken and appeared to be hardworking individuals who wanted to be regular American citizens.

"I'm worried about Rebekah, Asher. She is so naive and trusting. She hasn't had the same advantages to help her properly judge people. But you and I both know the Indians would like nothing better than to wipe out all traces of white settlements. Trying to force people here to accept the Indians will make her many enemies."

Asher looked down into her earnest face. It was sweet of Alexandra to be concerned about Rebekah's welfare, but she had misinterpreted the situation. This was not New Orleans. He often saw Indian families doing business with local merchants. "I hardly think taking a stroll with her neighbors would have such disastrous consequences."

"I'm worried about you, too, Asher. Papa says you have a brilliant career ahead of you, but your association with Rebekah could bring everything crashing down."

Now she was being downright foolish. Women had such a tendency to overdramatize. "I think you are making much ado over a very minor incident and drawing conclusions when you do not understand all the circumstances."

Alexandra turned her back to him and stared out of the window. "Please don't be angry with me. I have only your best interests at heart."

When Asher realized that her shoulders were hunched

forward, he felt like a villain. She was as young and as easily misled as Rebekah, but her heart was in the right place. "Don't worry, Alexandra. I'm not angry. But I do think you're assigning too much import to one instance."

"I pray you're right." Alexandra turned back toward him, her eyes large with unshed tears. "I only want to see you succeed."

As Alexandra looked up at him with such sincerity, Asher couldn't keep from wondering if Rebekah wanted success for him as well. Maybe it was time he found out.

&a.

Fearing that his frown was tensing the muscles between his eyebrows, Asher consciously forced a smile on his face as he looked around at the small group in Dolly Quinn's parlor.

Rebekah perched on the edge of the settee, one foot tapping a staccato rhythm beneath the folds of her skirt. Mrs. Quinn looked much more relaxed on the other end of the settee, sipping tea and nibbling at a strawberry scone. Rebekah's father stood with his back to the fireplace as he described yesterday's visit to the local smithy with his Indian friend, Wohali.

Asher nodded and tried to focus his attention on what the man was saying, but all he wanted to do was draw Rebekah away and talk to her. He had to be sure she had really forgiven him, even though he still wasn't certain what he had done. He wanted to have the right to pull her into his arms and tell her how much he loved her.

Asher kept his smile relaxed. It wouldn't do to let Rebekah know how hard his heart pounded. Was she ready to resume their plans for a future together? He could not bear the thought of her falling in love with someone else. She *had* to be reasonable and agree to remain in the city, where he could earn enough to support her.

Mr. Taylor ended his story, and silence filled the room.

Asher turned his attention once again to the girl he loved. "Rebekah, I hope you will dance with me at the Davis ball on Friday."

Her cheeks flushed, causing him to wonder if she was embarrassed by his statement or pleased at his attention.

"I'm sorry, but I doubt we'll still be here."

"Nonsense." Rebekah's aunt frowned and put down her teacup. "Your father knows how much I need you here. If you leave so soon, I will have to conclude that you no longer care for my company."

Rebekah's cheeks grew even redder, and Asher wished he had never opened his mouth. He had to rescue her. His mind searched frantically for a new topic. Something that would bring a smile to her face. "Have you heard that General Jackson has been given command of the southern division of the United States Army?"

Rebekah shook her head.

Excitement and pride filled Asher. "He's finally getting the recognition he deserves. He's a great man."

A commotion at the front door interrupted the conversation. Asher was surprised when Pastor Miller came rushing into the parlor.

"You have to leave. Quick!"

"Whatever is the matter, Pastor?" Mrs. Quinn asked. "Is something wrong?"

Asher had not been around the pastor much, but he recognized the man's perturbation in the way he glanced over his shoulder and wrung his hands together. He didn't even have the presence of mind to remove his hat.

The pastor shook his head and took a hurried breath. "There's been another Indian raid! Last night! They stole cattle and horses from the Marshall farm and burned down their cabin. No one can find the family. They're presumed dead."

His announcement was greeted with a small cry from Rebekah's aunt, who fell back against the settee. Rebekah grabbed a small brown bottle sitting on a table next to the settee and uncorked it. She sprinkled a few drops of pungent oil on her handkerchief and waved it below her aunt's nose.

As soon as Mrs. Quinn appeared to be recovering, the pastor continued. "I'm sorry for barging in with such distressing news, but I fear you are all in danger if we do not take quick action."

Asher turned his attention to the older man. "Why would Mrs. Quinn or her family be in any danger?"

"The townspeople seem to believe that Mr. Taylor's neighbor may have been involved." Pastor Miller finally remembered to remove his hat.

"But why would they think that?" Rebekah asked. "Wohali and Noya had nothing to do with any raid. They've been right here with us."

Asher left the other two men and came to where she sat with Aunt Dolly. "A mob won't be logical. They will want to hang any Indians they find."

The pastor nodded his agreement. "They're looking for scapegoats to bear the guilt for all the Indians."

Mr. Taylor stood and beckoned to the women. "I guess we should load up the wagon. We can hide both of them in the bed like we did when I first brought Rebekah here."

Asher pictured them meandering through Nashville on the lumbering wagon. "Do you think you can get away safely in a wagon?"

Pastor Miller crushed the brim of his hat with nervous fingers. "I think it would be better to take my buggy. It's much faster and has a fresh horse hitched to it. Five passengers will be a squeeze, but comfort is not our biggest concern."

"We can saddle a horse and tie it to the back of the buggy." Mr. Taylor looked out the front window while he considered the pastor's offer. "Then as soon as we get out of Nashville, Dolly or Rebekah can ride the horse."

Mrs. Quinn pushed herself into an upright position. "I'm not leaving my home."

Rebekah's father turned to her. "Don't be silly. A single woman is an easy target for an angry mob. We won't leave you to face them alone. You'll have to come with us."

Asher raised a hand to get Mr. Taylor's attention. "I'll stay behind and make sure no one hurts Mrs. Quinn or her home."

"I'll be here, too." Pastor Miller's mouth quirked upward. "After all, you'll be in my buggy."

"Thank you, Asher, Pastor." Mrs. Quinn nodded and sent a smile in his direction.

Asher straightened his shoulders. It was time to take charge. "We'll need to get that buggy out of here before there's real trouble. Mrs. Quinn, would you go and tell Wohali and his wife what's happened while Mr. Taylor and Pastor Miller get the buggy and the horses ready?" He hesitated a moment before turning to Rebekah. "Maybe you can show me where to find some extra blankets. We're likely to need something to help hide your passengers."

Rebekah's brown eyes had rounded, and he thought he could see a hint of admiration reflected in them. Good. It was time for her to understand that the boy she'd fallen in love with was a full-grown man, capable of dealing with any situation that arose. He followed her into the hallway, hoping to get a moment to tell her how much he still cared for her.

She opened a closet door and pulled at a tidy stack of wool blankets. "Will this be enough?"

As she turned to see his answer, Asher reached past her to help her hold the stack of blankets. Her forehead was barely an inch from his mouth. How he wanted to press a kiss against her soft skin—

A sound behind them jerked Asher's head up. He stepped

back and turned to find Wohali and his wife standing at the foot of the stairs. Their faces were expressionless, but he could feel heat burning his cheeks.

Rebekah shoved the quilts toward him. "Wohali, Noya, I'm so glad you're here. Did Dolly tell you what's going on?"

Asher could see the confusion in Noya's eyes. "We had nothing to do with the Indians who attacked those poor farmers. Why are they trying to hurt us?"

He felt Rebekah's gaze on him. Did she think he could explain the situation? The suspicions on both sides were deep and unyielding. But what answer could he give? He shrugged his shoulders.

Wohali looked down at his wife. "They are angry and frightened people who would not listen to us. It is the same with those of our tribe who blame all white men for the evil behavior of a few."

"Rebekah!" Mr. Taylor called to them from the back stairs. "Hurry up. We have to leave now."

Asher shifted his pile of blankets to one arm and held the other out for Rebekah to take, relieved when she rested her hand lightly on his forearm. Maybe she didn't realize how close he'd come to embarrassing both of them.

He led the way to the back door and the alley where Pastor Miller's buggy awaited them. Mr. Taylor was already seated in front and held the reins. Asher assisted Rebekah into the buggy beside her father before helping Pastor Miller tuck several quilts around Wohali and Noya, who had climbed into the back among sacks of potatoes and flour. They were fairly well concealed from a cursory glance, but he didn't know if it would fool anyone who came looking for scapegoats.

Pastor Miller stood to one side of the buggy, his head bowed. Asher could see his lips moving. He wished he could conjure up the words to a prayer, but nothing came to mind, so instead he watched mutely as Mr. Taylor prodded the horses and the buggy careened around a corner.

As they disappeared from sight and Asher heaved a sigh of relief at their escaping in time, the full extent of what he had done struck him. What if Rebekah's Indian neighbors had been involved in the massacre? Should he have encouraged Rebekah and her father to wait for the townspeople and turn Wohali over to them? He may have helped a murderer escape justice. If Colonel Lewis or General Jackson found out what he had done this afternoon, he would not be pleased.

But in the same instant, he acknowledged he would gladly risk a bit of their ire to have Rebekah look at him again with respect—and hopefully renewed love—in her eyes.

fourteen

Rebekah carried a heavy basket of wet clothing to the ropes Pa had rigged between two tulip poplars. The strong smell of Ma's lye soap made her nose wrinkle as she hung sheets and quilts to dry in the warm sunshine. She hummed as she wrung out a pillowcase and tossed it over the rope, enjoying the time alone.

She loved Eleanor, but her younger sister asked a lot of questions. What was it like in Nashville? Had she seen pirates in New Orleans? Was it fun to dance the night away in ballrooms? Was she going to marry Captain Landon? Ma had finally taken pity on Rebekah, sending her around to the side of the house to start drying the laundry while she and Eleanor finished the boiling and scrubbing.

The creak of a wagon turned Rebekah's attention from her task. She shaded her eyes, trying to make out who was coming to visit. She hoped it was not someone with more bad news. The trip from Nashville to Wohali's farm had been tense yesterday. She had been worried the whole time they would be attacked by either bloodthirsty Indian braves or enraged white settlers. It had been a relief to finally get home and stow Pastor Miller's buggy in the barn.

As the wagon drew nearer, she realized it was Pastor Miller returning her father's wagon. What a relief! He would be coming for his buggy and to report on what had happened yesterday after they escaped.

Rebekah picked up the last piece of wash and flung it over Pa's rope, making a note to herself to straighten it later. She then hurried to the front of the cabin, where the pastor was dismounting. "Welcome, Pastor Miller. What news do you bring?"

"Your aunt Dolly is fine. There were a few tense moments when the townspeople realized that all of you had left, but they dispersed after Captain Landon warned that their actions could put them in jail."

"That's wonderful news. So Asher. . .I mean Captain Landon. . .wasn't hurt either?" She could feel warmth in her cheeks at the mistake. It was one thing to refer to him by his given name when she was talking to her family—they all knew she and Asher had grown up together—but Pastor Miller might think she was being forward. He couldn't know that she and Asher had an agreement. Or at least they used to have an agreement. Maybe she should stop thinking of him as Asher. Their future together was no longer certain.

"The captain wasn't hurt." Pastor Miller smiled and put a hand on her shoulder. "He is a good man, Rebekah."

Rebekah realized the pastor might be able to help her with her confusion. "Yes, I think he is. But sometimes I worry about the other people in Nashville who seem to be influencing the way he thinks. He is always listening to that Colonel Lewis, and I don't know if he is a good example."

"I have seen the Lewis family in church upon occasion and have spoken with them. They seem to be nice folks who are close to General Jackson. Do you have some reason to worry about them?"

"Not exactly. Although they seem to support the removal of the Indians to the Western Territory." She looked up at him. "I don't like the idea of taking away their lands and homes."

"I applaud you for your sentiment, but I am afraid that there are many who would disagree with you. They point to events like the raid on the Marshall property to prove that we cannot allow the Indians to continue living among us."

"What do you believe, Pastor Miller?"

"I believe that we Christians have a duty to spread the gospel. God has given us a wonderful opportunity to show love and charity to a people who have never been exposed to His plan for salvation."

"I don't think Ash—Captain Landon would agree with you. He seems to be focused on advancing his career rather than his Christian duty."

"Why do you say that? He helped us get Wohali to safety, didn't he?"

Rebekah looked down at her apron. "Yes, but he often quotes Colonel Lewis and talks about the big fine house he wants to build. He won't listen to me when I tell him that a simple cabin will be sufficient."

"I think he is like most men." Pastor Miller rubbed his chin. "He wants to provide the best for the woman he loves."

"But what if that's not what I want?"

"Have you taken your worries to Jesus?"

Rebekah nodded. "I've prayed so hard that Asher would change back to the man he was before the war. Everything was easier then. He and I thought alike, and he listened to my hopes and dreams instead of telling me that I am being foolish or tenderhearted."

"Are you sure you thought exactly alike, Rebekah? Or did you misinterpret his dreams to make them match your own?"

She wanted to protest Pastor Miller's words. But what if he was right? Had she been mistaken about what Asher wanted? "I. . .I don't know." Her breath caught on a sob.

"You can never go back, but I believe you and Captain Landon can still have a future together if that's what God wants for you. Remember that you are God's beloved child. He wants the very best for you, and as long as you are willing to follow Him, you will find more blessings than you can imagine."

Rebekah wondered how this man could sound so sure of himself. He must have suffered disappointments and setbacks like anyone else. Yet faith flowed from him like a mighty current, sweeping all doubt away.

A small ray of hope broke through her confusion and worry. She would trust God to work it all out.

❧

Asher followed Colonel Lewis into the two-story log building that was General and Mrs. Jackson's home. The general had named his farm Rural Retreat but now called it The Hermitage, which meant the same thing. Asher had expected something more ostentatious for such a wealthy and important person, but this house was nearly as plain as the home in which he'd been raised and quite rustic when compared to the houses in Nashville.

The black house slave led them past a dining room that held at least a dozen chairs around a long plank table. They followed her to the door of the parlor to find the Jacksons engaged in prosaic activities, their chairs bracketing a bright window. He was perusing the newspaper while she embroidered a colorful design on a snowy white cloth.

Asher noticed the parlor walls had been covered with decorative paper that he supposed was nice. A round rag rug divided the room into two main parts—one side for leisure activities, the other side for business. The business side held a slightly smaller version of the dining-room table. On it stood a pair of candelabra, a scattering of maps and papers, and several haphazard stacks of books. A wooden armchair was situated on the far side of the desk, and a couple of simple stools on the other side stood ready for planning strategies.

General Jackson stood when they entered. "Rachel, I believe you know Colonel Lewis and his companion—"

Rachel Jackson interrupted her husband with a raised hand. "There is no need for you to introduce the dashing

Captain Landon. How pleasant to see you and Colonel Lewis. I trust our mutual acquaintance, Miss Rebekah Taylor, enjoys continued health."

Asher crossed the room and bowed over her hand. "She was in a bit of a hurry the last time I saw her, but I believe she is doing well."

"Yes, we heard about the commotion yesterday." Jackson frowned. "That's the main reason I invited you and the colonel over."

Rachel put away her needlework. "I believe I will take a short walk while you gentlemen have your discussion."

They waited until she left the parlor before taking their seats on either side of Jackson's desk. He pushed the candelabra and books to one corner and spread a map before them. "This is the location of an Indian village that may be hiding our culprits."

It took Asher a moment to get his bearings. The area outside Nashville was mostly wilderness, with small communities spread around it in an arc that followed the course of the Cumberland River. Jackson had his finger on a large longhouse shape that had been drawn at a curve in the river, indicating an Indian village. He moved his hand across an uninhabited area toward the land where Asher's parents had raised him. The hair on his neck stood on end when Asher realized the victims lived so close to the area in which he'd grown up. That meant they were very close to where Rebekah was right now.

"Everyone in Nashville is terrified, and the local authorities have asked for our help. You'll be working with the sheriff, but it will probably be up to you to find the culprits and bring them to justice."

Asher looked into Jackson's blazing eyes. "We'll find them, sir."

He held the older man's gaze for a minute or two before

Jackson nodded. "Good. Colonel Lewis said you were a true patriot."

Asher looked toward Colonel Lewis, who was still studying the map. "The colonel is very kind, sir. I was privileged to escort him and his family along the Natchez Road."

"You look familiar. I know you were a Tennessee militia-man, but have you performed some other service?" asked General Jackson.

"Yes, sir. You assigned me to be the liaison for William Weatherford."

"Ah, yes. Chief Red Eagle. Now I remember you. Good job you did on that assignment." Jackson rolled up the map. "No wonder the colonel speaks so highly of you. I can always use a man who quietly attends the business of his country. This is a matter of gravest importance. There are not many men who can accomplish the task I've set for you."

Asher's face heated as though he'd been outside farming. "Thank you, sir."

Colonel Lewis twirled his mustache. "Something has to be done about these Indians, Andrew."

The general's intense gaze left Asher's face and turned to the colonel. "Something is being done. I have already begun the process of drawing up a treaty between the government of the United States and the Cherokee Nation. While I sympathize with their wishes to retain their heritage and culture, it cannot be tolerated within the bounds of United States territory. They will either pledge their allegiance to our country, or they will leave it."

Asher's heart thumped in his chest like a drum. He realized he did agree with every word. This was an exciting time, a time when American supremacy was unquestioned. They had bought the right to expand westward with both their assets and their lives. Failure to demand absolute compliance from the Indian peoples would be nothing less than treason. God had smiled down on them by giving them this fertile land, and Asher would do everything in his power to ensure that his countrymen were allowed to fulfill their destiny.

"When I was about your age, Captain, I came west with little but the sense God gave me and a determination to succeed no matter the cost. I have never bowed to tyranny. Nor do I believe that our government should be controlled by the rich to the detriment of all free men. It is my duty and yours to uphold the words of America's Constitution."

"Quite right," said Colonel Lewis.

"Haven't we bled for our country?" Jackson banged his fist on the table. "Why then should we sit back and allow shortsighted politicians in the East to dictate how and where we shall govern ourselves?"

Asher snapped a salute, his back ramrod straight. He was in the presence of greatness. General Jackson was a man of integrity and a force of will that would never bow down. He was lucky to be able to work for him and hoped he could measure up to the general's expectations.

Rachel Jackson came back into the parlor. "I could hear you thundering all the way outside, husband. I thought surely you were being attacked by one of your visitors."

The fire in the general's eyes softened to admiration when he looked at his wife. It reminded Asher of the way he felt whenever Rebekah walked into a room. But he was glad she was not with him today. She might not have appreciated the general's words. Not that she wasn't a patriot. She was just tenderhearted.

He remembered when they were barely more than children and she had discovered a mockingbird that had fallen out of its nest. She had convinced him to help her nurse the bird back to health. When he'd been certain the mockingbird could survive on its own, Asher had met her at their tulip poplar, and they had set the bird free. He had comforted her while she cried, not exactly understanding her emotional outburst. Then he had shared her joy when the mockingbird returned in a few weeks to build a nest in their tree.

Even though she was now a full-grown woman, Rebekah was as compassionate as ever. She would never understand the necessity of freeing the Indians by sending them to a place where they could safely follow their heathen nature. He rubbed his hand on the back of his neck to distract himself from the voice whispering that there were Indians, like those he'd met at Rebekah's church, who could not be labeled heathens. Should they be forced to leave their homes, too?

Asher tried to force the voice to be silent, but its echo remained uncomfortably fixed in his heart even as he knew he must go forward to maintain his sought-after position.

fifteen

The next morning, Asher was up with the sun and anxious to get to Colonel Lewis's home. He dressed with haste and hurried through breakfast with his family. He would have liked to discuss with his pa how to proceed in the investigation, but given Pa's attitude about his new job, he decided to say nothing.

The streets were relatively quiet this early in the morning, and he made his way to the Lewis home without incident. Half expecting that the colonel had gathered a posse of angry men, Asher was thankful to discover no one awaiting his arrival.

He took the steps two at a time and banged his fist on the front door. An elderly black woman answered and led him toward the colonel's office. As he followed behind her, he wondered if the colonel would keep him waiting for long this morning.

"Come in, Captain." The colonel's voice answered his unspoken question. "I'm glad you arrived so early. I have been brought some evidence that will make our job much easier."

Asher shook the older man's hand. "That sounds promising. What kind of evidence?"

The colonel walked to his desk and picked up a brass-accented wooden writing box. "I considered sending a message to you last night when this was brought forward, but I decided it would be better to wait since we could not act upon it until daylight anyway."

"Who brought it?"

"Apparently the Marshalls had a farmhand who lived above

the stables and helped Mr. Marshall. As he knew I work for General Jackson, he came to me with this box."

Asher could hardly believe it. Someone had seen the raid? What wonderful luck. Now they would have descriptions of the culprits they were seeking. "How did he escape the attack?"

"He wasn't there. He'd been sent to Nashville for some provisions and decided to stay the night."

His explanation dashed Asher's hope for an eyewitness.

The colonel put the box in his hands and nodded at him to open it. Asher removed the wooden top and looked inside. His gaze registered the bloodstained Cherokee tomahawk while his imagination supplied the screams and pleas of the Marshall family before they died, as well as the coppery scent of their spilled blood.

"Where did he find this tomahawk?"

The colonel tapped his chin with one finger and looked toward the ceiling. "He went back the next morning to find the farmhouse and barns burned. He found the bodies of the Marshall family and decided to bury them. While he was working, he discovered the tomahawk lying on the ground near the place Mr. Marshall died. I can only surmise that it was dropped in the struggle."

Asher wanted to drop it right this minute. He had done his share of killing, but that had been his duty to his country, and it had been against men on the battlefield. He could not abide the images in his head of Mrs. Marshall and the children screaming in the night as they were mercilessly attacked by cold-blooded killers.

The colonel took the box from him. "There's one thing you may not have noticed."

Asher didn't want to have to look at the weapon again, but he steeled himself. "What's that?"

The older man reopened the box and withdrew the

tomahawk. "This is a fine piece. Not made by an Indian."

Asher was confused. "Indians didn't raid the Marshall farm?"

"I didn't say that." The colonel threw a smug look his way. "See the carved handle and steel blade? This is no crude weapon. It was probably made right here in Nashville by a white man."

"Then how did it—"

"I'm not sure, but my carriage has been brought around while I showed you the weapon. We're going to visit the craftsman this morning and find out." The colonel closed the writing box and locked it with a key, which he then pocketed. "And that information will likely lead us directly to the murderer."

It took the two men the balance of the morning to discover the designer of the tomahawk. He was a woodcarver who had a shop on the north end of Nashville. When they pulled up, the owner was sitting on a crude bench in front of the shop, whittling a large piece of white oak.

"Good morning, gents." The man smiled at them, exposing dark teeth with several gaps. "What can I do for you?"

Colonel Lewis stepped out of the carriage, his writing box tucked under one arm. "We're here to ask you about a tomahawk."

The man stood and leaned his work against the bench. "Come on in then. I've got plenty to choose from."

Asher walked inside, his gaze swinging around the room. Hundreds of handles hung on pegs all around the shop—some were smooth, while others had intricate designs carved on them. There were painted handles, leather-covered handles, and handles decorated with beads and feathers. Asher was amazed at the variety of styles to choose from.

"Are you looking for something fancy?"

"Not exactly." Colonel Lewis turned the key in his writing box and withdrew the bloody tomahawk. "We need to know if you carved this one."

The owner turned as pale as fresh snowfall. "Yep, it's one of mine. See the eagle's head I carved into the handle here? I. . .I sold this very tomahawk to a tall Indian who come in here with his squaw last week. He said he done broke his tomahawk and wanted somethin' special."

A look of satisfaction briefly replaced the man's alarm. "He came to me because he heard I'm the best there is. And he picked out this here one." He nodded at the weapon. "Said he 'specially liked the eagle on it."

Asher could barely contain his excitement. It had taken time and perseverance—and a bit of good fortune—but they had traced the weapon back to its source. Now all they had to do was find the Indian who'd bought it. He mused over the woodcarver's words, wondering if he should ask about a bill of sale. There had to be a clue. And then he knew. Like someone lifting a curtain to let bright sunshine into a dark room, the answer exploded into his consciousness. The Cherokees had a special word for the eagle—*wohali*. The woodcarver had to be describing Rebekah's new neighbor— the man he had helped escape justice. What had he done? Would his actions make her the next victim?

❦

Rebekah's ma laughed as she watched Noya punch her needle through the layers of her quilt patch, the force of her action nearly catapulting her from her rocker. "That's better, but you have to remember it's not as tough as a tanned hide."

The Indian woman smiled at her, pushing herself back before she overbalanced. "I know, but it seems to fight my needle."

"That's exactly why we came over." Rebekah stitched as she spoke, her needle moving up and down through the material. She loved sewing, watching as something came into being under her fingers.

That was especially true of quilts. Each square represented

a memory. Here was a square fashioned from an old dress of Ma's; there was one of Pa's wool vests. When they finished piecing all of the squares together, this quilt would tell a story about her family. And Noya's family as well, since several of the squares contained scraps donated from their old clothing.

Making the quilt had been Ma's idea. After the near disaster in Nashville earlier in the week, she had wanted to do something to show Wohali and Noya they were part of the community. And what better way than to work together on a project that both families had contributed to?

"You've made your home so charming." Ma squinted a little as she looked around the homey cabin. "I'm glad you bought it from Mrs. Winter's family after she passed away. She was a sweet lady, but we never seemed to have much in common. In the short time you've been here, we've already shared more recipes and stories than I ever did with Mrs. Winter."

Rebekah's gaze wandered around the small room. It was dominated by the kitchen area, complete with a wooden counter, a table with two benches, and a fireplace for cooking. In the far corner from the kitchen was the sleeping area. Someone had attached a raised sleeping platform to the wall and covered it with a colorful blanket. She wondered if Noya, who couldn't be five feet in height, had to use a stool to climb into it.

Much like her parents' cabin, there were windows on both sides of the door. They allowed sunlight and a fresh breeze into the cabin by day while their wooden shutters kept out the damp night air. A black bearskin rug had been placed in front of the door to prevent dirt and leaves from being tracked into the cabin. Dried apples hung from pegs that had been driven into the timber wall, along with berries and summer squash that would be used to supplement meals.

The hours flew by as the women sewed and chatted. After taking naps, Eleanor and Donny intermittently played inside and outside the cabin, carefully watched by the adults. When Pa and Wohali came in from the fields, it signaled the end of their party.

Before they could gather up their sewing notions, however, someone started banging on the front door of Wohali's cabin.

Rebekah looked at her parents. "Who can that be?"

Wohali snatched up his rifle and trained it on the door while placing himself between his wife and the disturbance. "I doubt it's good news."

"Open up."

Rebekah's heart leaped into her throat. She knew that voice. "Please wait! That's Asher." It must be a misunderstanding. She ran to the door and pulled it open.

Asher's jaw dropped when he saw her. "What are you doing here?" He grabbed her by the elbow and pulled her to him. "Have they hurt you?"

A part of her wanted to rest against him and listen to his heart beat, but she pushed herself away. "Of course not. Have you lost your senses? Ma and I came over to show Noya how to quilt while her husband and Pa were out digging a well because the creek has nearly dried up."

Pa pulled her back and faced Asher. "A better question would be what you are doing banging on the door like you're being chased by bandits."

Asher pointed past them at Wohali. "I've been sent to take Wohali into custody for the murders of the Marshall family."

Rebekah gasped. Had he been infected by the madness in Nashville? Or was this evidence of the very kind of influence she had worried about from the Lewis family? "What do you mean? You know they didn't have anything to do with that raid. They were with us at Aunt Dolly's house that night. How could he have been out at the Marshall place?"

Asher turned his gaze on her. Never had she seen him look so hard. His face seemed chiseled from stone, and his eyes looked straight through her. "A witness has come forward. We have enough evidence against Wohali, and you should be thankful for my arrival. You and your family may have been his next targets."

Rebekah's hand flew to her mouth. She glanced back at the Indian couple, who were standing close together. For an instant, she wondered if they could be capable of murder. But it was not possible. There was no way she would believe the woman she had spent the morning with could be in any way involved with the violent deaths of an innocent family.

She shook her head and turned to Pa. If Wohali harbored any evil intent, he would have seen evidence of it. "Pa, you can't let this happen."

Pa looked as shocked as she felt, but he shook his head. Was there nothing he could do to stop Asher from taking their neighbor?

Noya leaned up and whispered something to her husband, who turned his black gaze on Asher. "Who is this witness?"

"A farmhand. He got there too late to do anything to help the family. But the evidence he has is very convincing."

Rebekah could not, would not believe it. This was a gross miscarriage of justice. "There has to be a mistake."

"I wish there was, but you don't know all that I know—"

"I don't care what you think you know. It's simply not possible."

"Stay out of this, Rebekah. Someone found Wohali's tomahawk at the farm the next morning. There's no way it could have gotten out there unless he was a party to the murders. I know you have a soft spot for Indians, but you're allowing your feelings to cloud your judgment."

"At least I still have feelings." Her words fell into a well of silence. If possible she would have stuffed them back in her mouth. But it was too late.

Asher looked at her for a moment before shrugging. "I have

to do this no matter what you think of me." He shouldered his way past the others to face Wohali. "I'd like you to come peaceably. If what Rebekah says is right, we'll soon find out. But in the meantime, I have to take you to Nashville."

The Indian pried his wife's hands from his arms and nodded. "Do not worry, wife. God is in control." Without another word, he followed Asher into the yard.

Rebekah went to the short woman and hugged her tightly. "He's right, you know. Take heart. We'll straighten everything out in no time." Rebekah hoped to reassure herself with these words, but she knew she sounded much more certain than she actually felt.

sixteen

Asher took his prisoner to the jail. He was not happy with the way things had turned out. First, Rebekah's accusation that he was being heartless. Then Wohali's stoicism on the way back to Nashville.

The man had not put forward the least resistance, practically offering himself up as a sacrifice. Who did he think he was? Jesus? Asher's conscience pricked him. Was Wohali's silence an indication of innocence or guilt?

It was dusk, but he wanted to talk to Colonel Lewis about a couple of things. He hoped the man was at home, not escorting Alexandra and her ma to another ball. As his horse cantered across Nashville, Asher searched his memory for any invitations that his ma had mentioned, but he could not recall anything.

The Lewises must be at home, as nearly every window glowed against the deepening gloom. It was a very welcoming sight.

A stableboy came running to take care of his horse, and Asher climbed the front steps. How different the day had turned out than what he had been expecting when he first arrived at this very same doorway.

The same slave let him in. "I need to see the colonel again."

"Yes, sir." This time, she led him to a different part of the house, opening the door and announcing him to the people inside.

Asher entered the parlor, squinting at the sudden brightness. Alexandra was the first person he saw. She and her parents were enjoying tea in the parlor. Her smile was as wide and appealing as always. As she rose to meet him, Asher squelched a comparison between her and Rebekah. The last time he and Rebekah had disagreed, he had made that mistake, and he was determined not to repeat his error. Alexandra was nice, but his heart belonged to a stubborn, backward girl who was determined to rescue the world while dragging him away from a lucrative position in Nashville.

"To what do we owe this pleasure, Captain Landon?" She put out her hand for his kiss.

He bent and pecked at the air above her hand. "I have business with your father."

She pouted at him. "Is that the only reason you've come?"

"Alexandra!" Colonel Lewis's voice was sharp with censure. He left his easy chair and came over to stand next to his daughter. "You should mind your manners, young lady. It is unseemly of you to fish for a compliment."

Asher wondered why his shirt collar suddenly felt so uncomfortable. Although he agreed with the colonel, he did not like to witness Alexandra's discomfiture.

She looked down at the floor. "I'm sorry, Papa. I did not mean any harm."

Colonel Lewis's face lost its angry glower. He patted her shoulder. "No harm done, dear. Eh, Captain?"

Asher nodded his agreement and tugged at his collar. He turned to Alexandra's mother, who had remained seated on the sofa. "How do you do this evening?"

Mrs. Lewis sighed and waved a lacy kerchief. "As well as possible, I suppose, given the uncivilized nature of our surroundings."

Colonel Lewis cleared his throat. "Please remember that Captain Landon is from here, my dear. He probably doesn't agree with your disapprobation of Nashville."

"I would not dare to disagree with you, ma'am. I know you are more used to the comforts of a big city."

"Good answer." The colonel winked at Asher. "Perhaps we should retire to my study."

They left the ladies to their tea and headed down the hall.

"How did it go? Did you get the vermin?"

Asher winced at the colonel's choice of word. Before the evidence had been brought forward, he'd thought Wohali was an honorable man—hardworking, God-fearing, and honest. When he'd looked into Rebekah's eyes earlier, he had remembered that opinion. Had there been some mistake? "I'm worried about Wohali."

"Why? He murdered that poor defenseless family. He deserves whatever punishment we decide to mete out."

Asher sat down in one of the leather chairs. "I'm not sure he is guilty."

"Not guilty?" The colonel lifted a finger. "First, there's the bloody weapon, and then the description from the wood-carver of the man who purchased it. What more do you need? To see his hands coated with innocent blood?"

Asher leaned forward. "But can we be sure Wohali is the man who purchased the tomahawk? There are a lot of tall Indians around."

The colonel held his gaze for a moment. "If you're that worried about it, why don't you and I take this Indian to the woodcarver tomorrow and see if we've got the right person?"

Asher felt as though a weight had been lifted from his shoulders. "That's a good plan." Asking the woodcarver to identify Wohali would clear up his doubts, and he would be able to report to Rebekah that no mistake had been made. Surely then she would see the truth.

❧

Asher threw his pillow on the floor, relieved that the sky outside his bedroom window was finally beginning to lighten. It had taken him a long time to fall asleep last night, and he had not enjoyed his normal restful repose.

Haunting dreams had featured a disappointed Rebekah shaking her head and calling him heartless right before she was attacked by a wild-eyed Indian brave. No matter how hard he'd tried to save her from harm, by the time he reached her, she was dead. And when he turned to wreak vengeance on her attacker, the Indian faded into the shadows and disappeared.

He pushed back the bedcover and got up. One thing was for certain. Once all of this mess about the Marshall farm had been settled, he was going to Rebekah's home and ask for her pa's permission to marry. He had been foolish to put the matter off. That was the real reason Rebekah was unhappy with him. Never mind that he felt it was rushing things. If his Rebekah wanted to have their relationship formalized, he would do it.

So what if they had to live with his parents for a few months until he could put together enough resources to buy or build a home fitting the position they would hold? Look at Alexandra's relatives. Several married children lived with her grandmother at Tanner Plantation.

As he dressed, Asher got more and more excited about the idea of approaching Mr. Taylor. He couldn't think now why he had not done it sooner. He bounded down the stairs to tell his parents the exciting news before going to collect Wohali and Colonel Lewis. When he reached the first floor, however, he realized something was wrong. Several people were talking in the parlor.

He opened the parlor door to find the main participant in last night's dreams staring straight at him. "Rebekah! What's wrong? What are you doing here? Did someone attack your pa's farm?"

She was sitting between his parents on the sofa, her gloved hands clenching her reticule as though it held priceless treasure.

His ma stood up and gestured for Asher to take her place

on the sofa. "Miss Taylor has some important information I think you should hear." She smiled at Rebekah. "Mr. Landon and I will be in the dining room, dear. Call for us if you need anything."

As his parents left the parlor, Asher took the seat his ma had vacated. "What's wrong, Rebekah?"

Rebekah moved away from him a little. "What's wrong? Everything is wrong, Asher. The whole world has gone mad, and you with it. Pa brought me to town last night to try and avert disaster."

"What are you talking about?"

"I'm talking about you invading Wohali's home and dragging him away from his wife on some trumped-up charges that you know are not true."

Asher stiffened. "You don't know what you're talking about."

"I know there's no way that Wohali was involved in the murder of that poor family."

"You cannot know that."

She turned her gaze on him once more, her brown eyes pleading. "Asher, you know Wohali and Noya were staying with Aunt Dolly. Do you really think he sneaked out that night to murder the Marshalls and burn down their home before returning to Nashville and slipping back into his role as a civilized man?"

"I've seen a lot of things, Rebekah. A lot of things you don't need to know about. You've been protected from some of the harsh realities of life, and it's my intent to make sure you remain that way. Trust me when I say that a man can lose his grasp on civility in the blink of an eye. Even the best man can turn into a murderer under the right circumstances."

"But there are no circumstances that would compel Wohali to murder. I know him, and I know his wife. They are good Christian people who are trying to embrace our way of living.

Why would he suddenly decide to kill a bunch of strangers and put his whole future at risk?"

"I saw the evidence with my own eyes, Rebekah. I cannot give you a reason why Wohali would do anything so horrendous, but I know he did it."

Rebekah's eyebrows drew together. "You cannot know that."

Asher pried one of her hands from her reticule. "How can I make you understand the truth? Your innocence leads you to believe the best of people, but sometimes they don't deserve your trust. Do you know how scared I was when I realized that the weapon used to kill Mr. Marshall belonged to a man who lived next to you and your family? I must have died a thousand deaths on the way to Wohali's farm. I was so afraid that he might have turned his rage on you."

Rebekah jerked her hand away. "You have no need to worry about me anymore."

"Please, Rebekah, let's not start that same argument over again. You know I love you, and I know you love me. I promise you that I'm going to talk to your pa as soon as this is all—"

"Do not use that patronizing tone with me, Asher Landon. I'm not a child you can pat on the head and make empty promises to. I may have been protected by my loved ones, but that doesn't mean I'm stupid or easily misled. If anyone is being misled in this room, it's you. You are so blind you cannot see beyond your own nose. Noya has given me the only tomahawk that her husband owns."

Asher raised his eyebrows. "And you believe her?"

"Yes, I believe her. Coupled with the fact that Pa has worked side by side with Wohali for all these months and the fact that I know where he was that night, I have no doubt that Wohali is innocent. Instead of being so eager to believe that only Colonel Lewis and his daughter know the truth, why don't you ask yourself who might benefit from having Wohali arrested?"

If the situation had not been so serious, Asher would have laughed at the jealous comment she made. But it was serious. A man's life hung in the balance. "I cannot believe you think I am incapable of discerning the truth."

"And I can't believe you're not taking me seriously. Asher, I was willing to give you the benefit of the doubt. I was willing to believe that we could still have a happy marriage even if it meant I had to move to Nashville. But now I realize that you are not the man I thought you were."

"Rebekah—" Asher tried to break in, but her words struck him like blows, robbing him of breath. The expression on her face brought back his nightmare with vivid clarity.

"That's my fault, not yours. It's become obvious to me that there is a chasm between us which cannot be bridged. I was too self-centered to realize it earlier, and for that I do apologize. When Pastor Miller helped me realize that I had not been asking God for His leading, I turned to Him and asked for a sign that we were supposed to be together."

Asher had to be dreaming. That was it. That was why he couldn't make his tongue work—why he couldn't stem the flow of Rebekah's words.

"I guess the fact that you will not listen to reason is a pretty clear sign, so I want to formally release you from your promise." She stood up and walked across the room. "I pray you find your way to happiness."

❧

Rebekah rushed outside after her argument with Asher. She couldn't bear to face his parents. They were wonderful people, and they were worried about Asher, too, but she needed to be alone to get her emotions under control.

A sob nearly broke loose, but she choked it down. She climbed into Pa's wagon and grabbed the reins, turning the horse's head toward Aunt Dolly's home. As they traveled the streets of Nashville, the rhythmic sound of the wheels seemed to declare the verdict. . .over. . .it's over. . .over. . .it's over.

Her eyes stung, but she refused to let the tears fall. Was this how it was supposed to feel when one followed God's path? She could not believe Asher was truly lost to her. But since she'd left Nashville, he had gone even further down the path away from God. She could not join him there, even if it tore her heart out. She would collect Pa and go back home, and she hoped she would never have to set eyes on Nashville again.

A breeze caressed her cheek like a gentle hand, and peace settled inside her bruised heart. In that instant, she knew that their separation was necessary. Her heavenly Father knew what was best for all of them and she would trust His judgment.

As she neared her aunt's home, a song of thanksgiving filled Rebekah's mind, and she began to pray. She prayed for Wohali and for Noya, but most of all, she prayed that God would protect Asher and lead him into a bright future.

She felt her heart begin to break as she realized that future would not include her.

seventeen

Asher rode from the livery stable to the jail, leading Wohali's horse. But his mind wasn't on the Cherokee. It was on the scene with Rebekah.

After she had left, he tried to convince himself that it was for the best. He would go on with his life in Nashville, and she would live out in the country like she wanted. He would marry someone else, someone who respected him as a capable provider. Not someone who questioned every decision and tried to force him to bend to her will.

He would see Rebekah every now and then—when she came to visit her aunt, or when he had business in her area. Perhaps eventually they could even reclaim the friendship they'd once had. By then, he would probably have a couple of children, even if none of them sported her golden hair or soft brown eyes. Would she marry someone else? The pain that swept through him at the thought almost made him bend over his saddle.

She couldn't marry some other man. But if she didn't marry him, she would find someone else. . . .

He pushed the thought away. If he continued focusing on Rebekah, he would not be able to see things through for General Jackson and Colonel Lewis. And then he would lose both his love *and* his position.

The city was beginning to awaken as he reached the jail-house. Hitching both horses to the rail, he went inside and asked the sheriff to release the prisoner.

The sheriff stood up. He was taller than Asher and probably

outweighed him by a good thirty pounds. "Where are you wanting to take him?"

"Colonel Lewis and I are continuing our investigation under the direction of General Jackson."

The sheriff pulled out his ring of keys and walked over to Wohali's cell. "Make sure he doesn't plant a tomahawk in your scalp."

Asher rested a hand on his holster, glad he'd thought to buckle it on before leaving his parents' home. After the scene with Rebekah, it was a wonder he'd managed to do anything practical. "There's no danger of that."

Wohali looked the same as the day before. *Stoic* was the word that came to Asher's mind. The man's face could have been carved from stone.

Asher wished he could feel as unperturbed as Wohali seemed to be. He nodded at the Indian, who preceded him to the hitching post. He kept the reins of both horses in his hand as they headed for Colonel Lewis's home. "I trust the sheriff made sure your basic needs were met."

"The sheriff is a fair man."

They rode on in silence for a few moments, but Asher could not resist trying to break through Wohali's composure. "Are you curious about where we're going?"

"Do I seem curious to you?"

"No, but if I was in your place, I would be."

Wohali shrugged and turned his black gaze to the street. "You do not hold power over me."

Asher snorted. "I wouldn't be so sure about that. I'm about the only person in Nashville who wants to be sure you're guilty. If it were up to others, you would already feel the pinch of a noose around your neck."

Wohali glanced upward. "I answer only to my Lord and Savior. He knows my heart, and He alone will judge me."

Asher felt like he'd been slapped. He looked at the tall man who swayed to the rhythm of his horse. He felt small in comparison. How had that happened? He'd been certain he held the upper hand, but this Indian had put him to shame with a few simple words.

★

The woodcarver was not sitting outside when Asher and Colonel Lewis arrived with Wohali. Asher dismounted and stood at the horses' heads and waited while the colonel went in to get the man.

After a few minutes, he returned with the woodcarver. The colonel pointed at Wohali. "Is he the man who bought your tomahawk?"

"Yep, yep." The woodcarver wiped his hands on his pants. "That's the same one. Tall fellow, dark hair. That's the one alright." Another swipe of his palms on his trousers. "The very Indian that bought the tomahawk you fellows showed me t'other day. Yep, he's the one alright. Yep, yep. That's him."

Asher frowned. The woodcarver was not acting the way he had when they brought the tomahawk to him. He'd been calm then—proud of his craftsmanship and secure in his abilities. Today, he was exhibiting clear signs of extreme nervousness. He hadn't even looked at Asher. Or at Wohali. How could he be sure Wohali was the one who'd bought the tomahawk when he kept his head down and his gaze trained on the ground? He was also repeating himself again and again. Something was wrong.

Asher looked toward the colonel, but the older man didn't act as if anything was out of place. A glance toward the impassive Indian told him nothing.

The woodcarver was still talking about how they'd caught the right "varmint" and he'd be proud to be present at the hanging. Asher wanted to yell at him to quit talking. Every word he uttered convinced Asher that he was lying.

Rebekah's voice echoed in his head. *"Who might benefit from having Wohali arrested?"* Was this a conspiracy? If so, who were the conspirators?

eighteen

Sisters were a headache.

Asher wished he had never agreed to escort Mary to the dressmaker's, but he had been trying to mend fences with his family. They had been so cold and distant since that morning when Rebekah came to see him. Did they, like Rebekah, believe he was incapable of discerning the truth?

"Why, Captain Landon, I never expected to find you visiting a dressmaker." Alexandra's sultry voice interrupted his melancholy thoughts and brought a smile to Asher's face. She was dressed in a nice outfit—not that he knew much about women's clothing, but he thought the navy blue color made her eyes shine. And it had plenty of bows and lace. He knew from listening to his ma and sister that those types of notions made a dress more desirable.

He bowed and straightened. "What a pleasant surprise."

She breezed up to him, a smile on her face. "You say the kindest things, Captain. I'm so glad to run into you. I have the most exciting news—"

"Who are you talking to, Alexandra?" The colonel's bass tones were unmistakable. "Captain Landon!"

"Good morning, Colonel."

"Papa, I was just about to tell the captain about your decision to run for office."

Asher looked from one to the other, his mind in a whirl. "Run for office, sir?"

"Well, yes." Colonel Lewis lowered his voice, even though there were no other customers in the shop. "I guess it's acceptable to tell you, but I didn't want it bandied about just yet." He pointed a finger at Alexandra. "If I thought you were going to announce it to the whole world, young lady, I never would have told you."

"I'm sorry, Papa. But Asher is not the whole world." She put her hand on Asher's arm. "He's practically one of the family."

Asher could feel heat rush to his face. His initial pleasure at seeing Alexandra was drowned in embarrassment. While he enjoyed her friendly attention, being referred to as family was something else entirely. He refused to accept that things would not work out with Rebekah. She was the only family he wanted at this point.

He pulled his arm free from her grasp. "You are too kind, Miss Lewis." He turned to her pa. "Please be assured your news is safe with me."

Mary came out from the dressing room. She sized up the situation with a speed that pleased her brother. "Oh my, we're late for our appointment, Asher." She threw a smile in the general direction of the Lewises. "Please forgive me for dragging my brother away."

The next thing Asher knew, they were out the door. He breathed a sigh of relief. "That's the last time you will get me to go shopping with you."

Mary pouted at him. "And here I thought I'd rescued you handily."

"Maybe so, but I wouldn't have needed rescuing if you hadn't dragged me into that shop in the first place." Asher helped her into the carriage and looked around to make sure Alexandra hadn't decided to pursue him. Something about Alexandra's announcement was bothering him. He looked up at the driver. "Take Mary back home, and do not let her talk you into stopping anywhere else."

"Aren't you coming with me, Asher?"

Asher shook his head. "Tell Ma I'll be back later. I need to do some thinking."

She started to say something, but he closed the carriage door on her protest. As the driver pulled out into the busy street, he wandered in the other direction, his mind in a whirl. Why had Colonel Lewis suddenly decided to run for office? And why hadn't he told Asher himself? Why try to keep it a secret? It made no sense to him at all.

Asher was surprised to look around and find himself back at the woodcarver's shop. It looked different today. All the windows had been shuttered, and the carver's bench was no longer sitting on the front porch.

Curious, he climbed the steps and knocked on the front door. It swung open as a result of his knock. "Hello? Is anyone here?"

He walked inside and looked around, his mouth falling open in shock. All the handles that had been hanging on the walls last week were gone. Not a single one remained. The only things left inside the store were a broom and a broken chair.

"What are you doing in here?"

The belligerent voice behind him startled Asher, and he spun around to find the woodcarver outlined in the doorway. "I found myself in the area and decided to stop by."

The woodcarver grunted. "I'm closed."

"I can see that. It looks like you're not planning on reopening."

"I came into some money, so I decided to close down this two-bit operation and open up a store in Philadelfy."

Asher nodded. "Do you have family back there?"

"What business is it of yours, Captain?" The woodcarver's voice was challenging.

Asher spread his hands. "None whatsoever. My only business with you concerns the Indian, Wohali. You will be here until after the trial is over, right?"

"I don't know." The woodcarver dropped his gaze and rubbed a hand on the leg of his pants. The same nervous gesture Asher had noted during his second visit. "I. . .I've got me a real hankering to move away."

"But without your testimony, the murderer might go free."

The woodcarver shrugged. "I don't rightly want to go swear as to selling that tomahawk to your Indian."

Asher's jaw dropped. "You told me and the colonel that you sold it to Wohali, so why would you be hesitant to testify in court? Unless you were lying. . ."

Another shrug was the only answer.

Asher's heart banged in his chest. "If you were lying, you must have a real good reason." A plausible motive occurred to him. "Were you part of the raid that killed that poor family?"

The woodcarver looked at him again, and now Asher could see his fear. "I didn't kill nobody."

Asher decided to push him a little. "And why should I believe that? Guilt is usually what makes men run away."

"You got it all wrong, Captain. I promise you I didn't kill those folks. I just make the weapons 'cause God give me a talent for it."

"If you didn't kill anybody, why would you lie about who bought the tomahawk?"

"I come in here one morning, and it was gone. Somebody stole it."

Asher blew out a breath of disgust. "Come on and try another tale. But this time, try to make it plausible."

The man cringed.

"I'm running out of patience." Asher tapped his foot. "Who bought the tomahawk?"

"If I tell you that, they'll come back and kill me."

Asher pointed a finger at the woodcarver. "If you don't tell me, I am going to drag you to jail and throw you into the cell with Wohali. Then we'll see what's what."

"No." The man looked back over his shoulder. "Look, I'll tell you, but you've gotta promise that you won't say anything until I get outta here."

"I can't make that promise." Asher strode forward and grabbed the man's elbow. "Why don't we go see Colonel Lewis? Maybe he'll convince you to tell the truth."

The woodcarver struggled to break free of Asher's hold. "No, you can't take me there. He'll kill me for sure."

Asher twisted to block the doorway. "What are you saying? Are you trying to implicate Colonel Lewis? Did you sell him the tomahawk?" His mind reeled. But it made sense. The facts lined up with military precision. The colonel was planning to grab Wohali's and the Marshalls' land. Only substantial landowners could hold public office. It didn't matter whether he lived on the land or not, so long as he held the title.

The woodcarver was sniveling, his misery plain to see. "I didn't do nothing wrong. You've got to believe me. I sold it to him, but I thought he was going to use it for some ceremony, not to kill them folks. And when I found out, it was too late. The colonel came here and told me to say I'd sold it to an Indian. He said them Indians was all guilty on account of they've killed lots of white men. And he said he'd pay me big. All I had to do was agree with him—then I could leave Nashville, and everyone would be okay."

Asher's whole world changed in that instant. Colonel Lewis, the man in whom he had placed so much faith, was pure evil. He'd been such a fool. Everything he'd thought was right had turned out to be wrong, terribly wrong.

All this time he had refused to listen to his loved ones. They had tried to warn him, but he'd been certain he was right. He'd let his ambitions blind him to the truth. He knew without a doubt that he was nothing more than a flawed sinner. Asher wanted to sink to his knees on the dusty floor and beg for God's forgiveness. But he didn't have that choice. He had to stop the colonel before Wohali paid the ultimate price for Asher's stupidity. He could only ask God to help him until he could really seek peace later. "Come on. We're going to the sheriff."

The woodcarver shook his head and tried to get through the doorway, but Asher tackled him. "No you don't. You're through running from shadows. It's time to stand up and be a man." He hustled the frightened man down the street toward the jail and dragged him inside.

The sheriff looked up when they entered. "Who are you bringing in today, Captain?"

"This man has an interesting story to tell you, Sheriff. I think you and Wohali are going to want to listen."

He tossed a glance toward the Indian, who was sitting quietly in his cell. The woodcarver faltered at first, but he told his story once again.

When he finished, the sheriff looked at Asher. "Do you believe him?"

Asher lifted his chin toward the broken man. "Look at him. He's scared to death. Too scared to lie."

The sheriff nodded. "I agree." He stood and walked to Wohali's cell and turned the key in the lock. "I guess we'd better get you out of here."

The front door flew open and banged against the wall. "Don't anybody move."

"Colonel Lewis." Asher reached for his holster before realizing he'd not strapped it on that morning. He'd never dreamed he might need a weapon on a shopping excursion.

The colonel, however, had brought his weapon, and he pointed it at Asher. "Get back, boy. I don't want to hurt you. My daughter's got a soft spot for you."

Asher's jaw dropped. "Please tell me you haven't embroiled her in this sordid mess."

"Don't be ridiculous. This is men's business. I wouldn't think of even telling her about it." He barked a humorless laugh. "Just look at the way she said too much to you today and roused your suspicions."

Out of the corner of his eye, Asher could see the sheriff easing his way back to his desk. He needed to distract Colonel Lewis if any of them were going to get out of this alive.

"Is that the way they do business in New Orleans? Murdering innocent women and children?"

The colonel shrugged. "They were in the way. I need all of that land from the river to the Taylor farm for my purposes. That idiot wouldn't sell to me. Said he'd planted roots there. So I had him planted there with his roots."

He pulled back the hammer and pointed his gun at the woodcarver. "I told you to keep your mouth shut or you'd end up like that farmer."

Asher could not let the terrified man be killed. He leaped toward the colonel and shoved the older man's arm hard. A double blast filled the jail with smoke and the smell of burned powder. The colonel let out a groan and fell dead at Asher's feet.

Asher looked down at himself, surprised to see that he was not leaking blood. He looked at the woodcarver, who was staring in horrified fascination at the other end of the room. The sheriff! He turned in time to see the tall man fold in half and land on the floor with a *thump*.

He hurried to the sheriff and turned him over to see a nasty wound a slight distance from the man's heart. Someone knelt beside him. It was Wohali.

"I can take care of the bleeding. You get the doctor." Wohali inclined his head to the body of Colonel Lewis. "No one else should die because of that man's greed."

"Wohali, I don't know what—"

The sheriff's groan cut off Asher's apology.

"Go now." The Indian pressed his hand against the wound. "We can talk later."

nineteen

Rebekah pulled off her shoes and stockings and thrust her feet into the cold stream. A sorrowful sigh seemed to fill her chest, and tears gathered at the corners of her eyes. "I will not cry. I will not cry. I will not—"

A chirp in the limb above her head stopped her words. She looked up to see the gray brown feathers of a mockingbird. Its song continued, full of chiding tweets.

She frowned. "Are you mocking me?"

"Perhaps. But she is more likely trying to warn you away from the babies in her nest."

Rebekah's breath caught, and she drew her legs out of the water so she could turn around. There he stood—so tall, so handsome, so much the man of her dreams. *Asher.* "What are you doing here?"

"I came to ask for your forgiveness." He reached for her hand and drew her up. Rebekah's petticoat clung to her damp, bare legs. She took one step to the right, hoping to hide her shoes and stockings from his view. How embarrassing to be caught dangling her bare feet in the water like a child. She would have liked to leave him standing beside the creek, but she could not move without exposing her undergarments.

"I forgive you, Asher." She looked down to be certain her bare toes were not peeking out.

He put a hand under her chin and raised her face to look at him. "No, not yet."

All thoughts of her feet slid out of Rebekah's head.

His blue eyes captured her whole attention. He looked so uncertain, so anxious. "Did you know that Wohali has been released? He is completely exonerated."

Rebekah nodded. Wohali had come home a week ago. Her family had celebrated the release with great joy. He'd told them about Asher's part in uncovering Colonel Lewis's devious plan. He'd described the woodcarver's confession and the gunfight, almost causing her to experience an Aunt Dolly swoon at the thought of Asher being shot down in the city jail.

Another detail he shared with them was the departure of the widowed Mrs. Lewis and Alexandra. They had decided to return to the family plantation rather than face the scandal surrounding the colonel's reprehensible actions. Rebekah could not imagine the grief and pain Alexandra must be experiencing and found herself praying often for God's comfort and peace to surround her former rival.

Asher's hand reached back to tuck a stray lock of hair behind her ear. "I cannot believe what a fool I've been, Rebekah. I should have listened to you. You saw everything more clearly than I did. You were right when you accused me of being heartless. I had let myself be misled by promises of glory and wealth. But I hope you know that I had no idea what means the colonel had in mind to achieve those goals."

"Of course I believe that, Asher. I never thought you were a criminal."

"Thank you. When I look back on my words and actions, I couldn't blame you if you didn't believe me." He paused for a moment and gazed over her shoulder. "When I discovered what really happened at the Marshall farm that night, I was devastated. This bright light seemed to bear down on me, and it made me so ashamed. I wanted to run from the truth, but there was nowhere to hide. God let me see how far from Him I'd gone. I died in that moment, Rebekah."

She put a hand on his arm. "I'm so sorry."

"No." He shook his head and focused on her again. "Don't

be sorry. Be glad. I know I've been foolish, Rebekah. When I told my parents how sorry I was, Pa suggested I go talk to Pastor Miller. He's a very smart man. He and I talked a long time. When I told him how I felt, he read to me about Isaiah's vision of God. 'Woe is me! for I am undone; because I am a man of unclean lips. . . .' Knowing that one of God's prophets had felt the same gave me hope that I could change in spite of the terrible things I had done. I feel like Paul—ashamed that I have spent so much time doing the wrong things but full of joy that I can now spend my energies on pleasing Him."

Rebekah could not see him struggling so without feeling a deep pathos for Asher. Yet underlying that sadness was an upwelling of joy. Was it possible that he had changed in an instant? Yet hadn't her own views changed that fast because of the face of an Indian boy on the road from Natchez? "Oh, Asher."

"I hope you understand, Rebekah. I'm not only asking for your forgiveness for my past errors. I want you to take me back." He dropped to one knee in front of her and took her hand in both of his. "I have put God first in my life, and I feel that He has led me to this moment. Can you ever love me again?"

Rebekah laughed. She could not help herself. All the sorrow that had weighed her down for weeks was gone as if it never existed. "Although I was resigned to life without you, it was so hard to forget how much you meant to me. I kept thinking I should be doing more to reach you, but I didn't know how to accomplish it. So I prayed."

"Thank you, Rebekah. I am not worthy of such dedication."

"Please get up, Asher." She tugged on the hands that enveloped hers. "You don't need to humble yourself to me. 'For all have sinned, and come short of the glory of God.' Everyone needs God's grace and forgiveness."

"Does that mean you'll marry me?"

She laughed again. "Well, you still haven't asked Pa...."

"I can take care of that detail right now. But first..." Asher sprang to his feet and wrapped his arms around her.

Rebekah reveled in the feel of his strong arms and sent a prayer of thanksgiving heavenward. The Asher she'd grown up loving had come back to her. His sincere remorse was plain to see in his face. She no longer had to worry that he would sacrifice her happiness or his relationship with God for fame and fortune. As he held her close, she felt safe and finally at peace. Her heart skipped a beat when he gently bent his head and kissed her.

She felt God's love surround them and give their relationship a wonderful new aspect. It was deeper and richer than before. Somehow, she knew that this was the way God intended for His children to come together, and she could hardly wait to begin their journey along His path.

· epilogue

Mid–October 1815

Donny came running into the room and pulled on the skirt of Rebekah's dress.

She pulled him onto her lap. "Yes, dear. What's wrong?"

"Ma says come on. Ev'one waiting."

Rebekah lifted her little brother off of her lap and stood. As he ran back outside, she brushed the pale yellow material of her gown. It was the first one Aunt Dolly had given her. . .and her favorite. She had known it would be the perfect choice to begin her new life.

Rebekah opened the door and stepped into the bright autumn sunshine. She sent a quick prayer heavenward, thanking God for providing such a beautiful day for the moment she would become Mrs. Asher Landon.

"Here she is." Pastor Miller's voice turned everyone's attention to her. He was standing beside Asher under the shade of the tulip poplar, which seemed to have dressed especially for her wedding as the beginnings of fall colors showed in its leafy branches.

She walked past the grand table Pa had hewn from the trunk of a gigantic tree. When she had first seen it, she'd not been able to imagine that they could fill the table with food, but it now practically groaned underneath the weight of everything from cakes and pies to roast chicken, duck, and venison. As soon as Pastor Miller invoked God's blessing on her union to Asher, they would all sit around Pa's table and fellowship together.

She smiled at Wohali and Noya. They were being better received since the truth about the Marshall tragedy had been uncovered. The Cherokee couple's steadfast faith during Wohali's imprisonment had even won over several of her neighbors who did not normally like to associate with Indians.

Asher's family was standing next to the creek, to his right, while Rebekah's family stood on the other side of Pastor Miller.

Una Miller had claimed one of the chairs Pa had moved out from the cabin. She sat next to Rachel Jackson, who cooed over the precious baby girl Mrs. Miller cradled in her arms. Even the general was smiling as he bent over his wife. Aunt Dolly was standing next to the sheriff, whispering something in his ear as she waved a lace handkerchief at Rebekah.

Then all Rebekah's attention centered on Asher standing so tall and handsome in his uniform. It was a shame he would not don it again after today's ceremony, but he had decided to resign from the militia and take a job at his pa's bank. The only reason he wore it for the wedding was because General and Mrs. Jackson were present.

Asher had also joined her in talking with Pastor Miller about working with the Indians in the area. They would help to educate them so they would be able to adapt to the changes on the frontier. But more importantly, they would work together to tell the Indians of God's love and forgiveness, available to *all* of His children.

It seemed to Rebekah she had waited for this moment for half a lifetime, but she could not regret the delay because she knew instinctively that she and Asher had not been ready to begin a marriage two years ago—not until they put their lives fully in God's hands. She prayed they were ready now.

Together they faced Pastor Miller, who smiled as he opened his Bible. " 'And the Lord God said, It is not good that the man should be alone; I will make him an help meet for him.' Friends, I give you today Asher Landon, a good man who has come to me many times over the past weeks, seeking the will of God. He has promised to cherish and care for Rebekah Taylor. . . ."

Rebekah let the words wash over her. She looked at the man who was becoming her husband and felt a great peace flow through her. Here under their tulip poplar, all of their dreams were coming true.

A Letter To Our Readers

Dear Reader:
In order that we might better contribute to your reading enjoyment, we would appreciate your taking a few minutes to respond to the following questions. We welcome your comments and read each form and letter we receive. When completed, please return to the following:

Fiction Editor
Heartsong Presents
PO Box 719
Uhrichsville, Ohio 44683

1. Did you enjoy reading *Under the Tulip Poplar* by Diane Ashley and Aaron McCarver?
   ❑ Very much! I would like to see more books by this author!
   ❑ Moderately. I would have enjoyed it more if

   _____

   _____

   _____

2. Are you a member of **Heartsong Presents**? ❑ Yes ❑ No
   If no, where did you purchase this book? _____

   _____

3. How would you rate, on a scale from 1 (poor) to 5 (superior), the cover design? _____

4. On a scale from 1 (poor) to 10 (superior), please rate the following elements.

   ____ Heroine   ____ Plot
   ____ Hero   ____ Inspirational theme
   ____ Setting   ____ Secondary characters

5. These characters were special because? _____

_____

_____

6. How has this book inspired your life? _____

_____

_____

7. What settings would you like to see covered in future
   Heartsong Presents books? _____

_____

_____

8. What are some inspirational themes you would like to see
   treated in future books? _____

_____

_____

9. Would you be interested in reading other **Heartsong
   Presents** titles? ❑ Yes   ❑ No

10. Please check your age range:
     ❑ Under 18   ❑ 18-24
     ❑ 25-34   ❑ 35-45
     ❑ 46-55   ❑ Over 55

Name _____

Occupation _____

Address _____

City, State, Zip_____

UNDER THE BIG SKY

3 stories in 1

Take a journey back to Montana's early days and watch as faith and love flourish through three generations.

Historical, paperback, 352 pages, 5⁵⁄₁₆" x 8"

Please send me _____ copies of *Under the Big Sky*. I am enclosing $7.97 for each. (Please add $4.00 to cover postage and handling per order. OH add 7% tax. If outside the U.S. please call 740-922-7280 for shipping charges.)

Name_____

Address _____

City, State, Zip _____

To place a credit card order, call 1-740-922-7280.
Send to: Heartsong Presents Readers' Service, PO Box 721, Uhrichsville, OH 44683

Heart♥ong

Any 12
Heartsong
Presents titles
for only
$27.00*

HISTORICAL ROMANCE IS CHEAPER BY THE DOZEN!

Buy any assortment of twelve *Heartsong Presents* titles and save 25% off of the already discounted price of $2.97 each!

*plus $4.00 shipping and handling per order and sales tax where applicable.
If outside the U.S. please call 740-922-7280 for shipping charges.

HEARTSONG PRESENTS TITLES AVAILABLE NOW:

___HP619 *Everlasting Hope*, T. V. Bateman	___HP688 *A Handful of Flowers*, C. M. Hake
___HP620 *Basket of Secrets*, D. Hunt	___HP691 *Bayou Dreams*, K. M. Y'Barbo
___HP623 *A Place Called Home*, J. L. Barton	___HP692 *The Oregon Escort*, S. P. Davis
___HP624 *One Chance in a Million*, C. M. Hake	___HP695 *Into the Deep*, L. Bliss
___HP627 *He Loves Me, He Loves Me Not*, R. Druten	___HP696 *Bridal Veil*, C. M. Hake
___HP628 *Silent Heart*, B. Youree	___HP699 *Bittersweet Remembrance*, G. Fields
___HP631 *Second Chance*, T. V. Bateman	___HP700 *Where the River Flows*, I. Brand
___HP632 *Road to Forgiveness*, C. Cox	___HP703 *Moving the Mountain*, Y. Lehman
___HP635 *Hogtied*, L. A. Coleman	___HP704 *No Buttons or Beaux*, C. M. Hake
___HP636 *Renegade Husband*, D. Mills	___HP707 *Mariah's Hope*, M. J. Conner
___HP639 *Love's Denial*, T. H. Murray	___HP708 *The Prisoner's Wife*, S. P. Davis
___HP640 *Taking a Chance*, K. E. Hake	___HP711 *A Gentle Fragrance*, P. Griffin
___HP643 *Escape to Sanctuary*, M. J. Conner	___HP712 *Spoke of Love*, C. M. Hake
___HP644 *Making Amends*, J. L. Barton	___HP715 *Vera's Turn for Love*, T. H. Murray
___HP647 *Remember Me*, K. Comeaux	___HP716 *Spinning Out of Control*, V. McDonough
___HP648 *Last Chance*, C. M. Hake	___HP719 *Weaving a Future*, S. P. Davis
___HP651 *Against the Tide*, R. Druten	___HP720 *Bridge Across the Sea*, P. Griffin
___HP652 *A Love So Tender*, T. V. Batman	___HP723 *Adam's Bride*, L. Harris
___HP655 *The Way Home*, M. Chapman	___HP724 *A Daughter's Quest*, L. N. Dooley
___HP656 *Pirate's Prize*, L. N. Dooley	___HP727 *Wyoming Hoofbeats*, S. P. Davis
___HP659 *Bayou Beginnings*, K. M. Y'Barbo	___HP728 *A Place of Her Own*, L. A. Coleman
___HP660 *Hearts Twice Met*, F. Chrisman	___HP731 *The Bounty Hunter and the Bride*, V. McDonough
___HP663 *Journeys*, T. H. Murray	___HP732 *Lonely in Longtree*, J. Stengl
___HP664 *Chance Adventure*, K. E. Hake	___HP735 *Deborah*, M. Colvin
___HP667 *Sagebrush Christmas*, B. L. Etchison	___HP736 *A Time to Plant*, K. E. Hake
___HP668 *Duel Love*, B. Youree	___HP740 *The Castaway's Bride*, S. P. Davis
___HP671 *Sooner or Later*, V. McDonough	___HP741 *Golden Dawn*, C. M. Hake
___HP672 *Chance of a Lifetime*, K. E. Hake	___HP743 *Broken Bow*, I. Brand
___HP675 *Bayou Secrets*, K. M. Y'Barbo	___HP744 *Golden Days*, M. Connealy
___HP676 *Beside Still Waters*, T. V. Bateman	___HP747 *A Wealth Beyond Riches*, V. McDonough
___HP679 *Rose Kelly*, J. Spaeth	___HP748 *Golden Twilight*, K. Y'Barbo
___HP680 *Rebecca's Heart*, L. Harris	___HP751 *The Music of Home*, T. H. Murray
___HP683 *A Gentleman's Kiss*, K. Comeaux	___HP752 *Tara's Gold*, L. Harris
___HP684 *Copper Sunrise*, C. Cox	___HP755 *Journey to Love*, L. Bliss
___HP687 *The Ruse*, T. H. Murray	

(If ordering from this page, please remember to include it with the order form.)

Presents

___HP756 *The Lumberjack's Lady*, S. P. Davis
___HP759 *Stirring Up Romance*, J. L. Barton
___HP760 *Mountains Stand Strong*, I. Brand
___HP763 *A Time to Keep*, K. E. Hake
___HP764 *To Trust an Outlaw*, R. Gibson
___HP767 *A Bride Idea*, Y. Lehman
___HP768 *Sharon Takes a Hand*, R. Dow
___HP771 *Canteen Dreams*, C. Putman
___HP772 *Corduroy Road to Love*, L. A. Coleman
___HP775 *Treasure in the Hills*, P. W. Dooly
___HP776 *Betsy's Return*, W. E. Brunstetter
___HP779 *Joanna's Adventure*, M. J. Conner
___HP780 *The Dreams of Hannah Williams*, L. Ford
___HP783 *Seneca Shadows*, L. Bliss
___HP784 *Promises, Promises*, A. Miller
___HP787 *A Time to Laugh*, K. Hake
___HP788 *Uncertain Alliance*, M. Davis
___HP791 *Better Than Gold*, L. A. Eakes
___HP792 *Sweet Forever*, R. Cecil
___HP795 *A Treasure Reborn*, P. Griffin
___HP796 *The Captain's Wife*, M. Davis
___HP799 *Sandhill Dreams*, C. C. Putman
___HP800 *Return to Love*, S. P. Davis
___HP803 *Quills and Promises*, A. Miller
___HP804 *Reckless Rogue*, M. Davis

___HP807 *The Greatest Find*, P. W. Dooly
___HP808 *The Long Road Home*, R. Druten
___HP811 *A New Joy*, S.P. Davis
___HP812 *Everlasting Promise*, R.K. Cecil
___HP815 *A Treasure Regained*, P. Griffin
___HP816 *Wild at Heart*, V. McDonough
___HP819 *Captive Dreams*, C. C. Putman
___HP820 *Carousel Dreams*, P. W. Dooly
___HP823 *Deceptive Promises*, A. Miller
___HP824 *Alias, Mary Smith*, R. Druten
___HP827 *Abiding Peace*, S. P. Davis
___HP828 *A Season for Grace*, T. Bateman
___HP831 *Outlaw Heart*, V. McDonough
___HP832 *Charity's Heart*, R. K. Cecil
___HP835 *A Treasure Revealed*, P. Griffin
___HP836 *A Love for Keeps*, J. L. Barton
___HP839 *Out of the Ashes*, R. Druten
___HP840 *The Petticoat Doctor*, P.W. Dooly
___HP843 *Copper and Candles*, A. Stockton
___HP844 *Aloha Love*, Y. Lehman
___HP847 *A Girl Like That*, F. Devine
___HP848 *Remembrance*, J. Spaeth
___HP851 *Straight for the Heart*, V. McDonough
___HP852 *A Love All Her Own*, J. L. Barton
___HP855 *Beacon of Love*, D. Franklin
___HP856 *A Promise Kept*, C. C. Putman

Great Inspirational Romance at a Great Price!

Heartsong Presents books are inspirational romances in contemporary and historical settings, designed to give you an enjoyable, spirit-lifting reading experience. You can choose wonderfully written titles from some of today's best authors like Wanda E. Brunstetter, Mary Connealy, Susan Page Davis, Cathy Marie Hake, Joyce Livingston, and many others.

When ordering quantities less than twelve, above titles are $2.97 each.
Not all titles may be available at time of order.

SEND TO: **Heartsong Presents** Readers' Service
                P.O. Box 721, Uhrichsville, Ohio 44683

Please send me the items checked above. I am enclosing $ _____
(please add $4.00 to cover postage per order. OH add 7% tax. WA add 8.5%). Send check or money order, no cash or C.O.D.s, please.
To place a credit card order, call 1-740-922-7280.

NAME _____

ADDRESS _____

CITY/STATE _____ ZIP _____

HPS 8-09

HEARTSONG
P R E S E N T S

If you love Christian romance…

$10.⁹⁹

You'll love Heartsong Presents' inspiring and faith-filled romances by today's very best Christian authors…Wanda E. Brunstetter, Mary Connealy, Susan Page Davis, Cathy Marie Hake, and Joyce Livingston, to mention a few!

When you join Heartsong Presents, you'll enjoy four brand-new, mass-market, 176-page books—two contemporary and two historical—that will build you up in your faith when you discover God's role in every relationship you read about!

Imagine…four new romances every four weeks—with men and women like you who long to meet the one God has chosen as the love of their lives…all for the low price of $10.99 postpaid.

To join, simply visit www.heartsong presents.com or complete the coupon below and mail it to the address provided.

Mass Market 176 Pages

YES! Sign me up for Heartsong!

NEW MEMBERSHIPS WILL BE SHIPPED IMMEDIATELY!
Send no money now. We'll bill you only $10.99 postpaid with your first shipment of four books. Or for faster action, call 1-740-922-7280.

NAME _____

ADDRESS_____

CITY_____ STATE _____ ZIP _____

MAIL TO: HEARTSONG PRESENTS, P.O. Box 721, Uhrichsville, Ohio 44683
or sign up at **WWW.HEARTSONGPRESENTS.COM**